Legends of THAMATURGA
The Traveler

To my family whom I love dearly. Without you, I would not have ventured to write this story.

To my sister, without her help and encouragement I would not have finished.

To my fans, I hope you enjoy this adventure.

Prologue

The world was plainer back then. No difference, no wonder. The elderly man stepped off his boat and onto what he thought was another deserted island. He was surprised when he was greeted by a tribe of midgets. They were colorful and exotic. Varying in skin shades from blue to green to purple and pink. The man was awed by the diversity of the small group. He was invited to sit with them for a spell where they offered to teach him what they knew. The man graciously agreed for knowledge was what he sought. At the end of his stay he offered them gifts. Items he had collected on his travels. The people asked for more. The elderly man obliged. He in turn gave to them all he had, his blankets, his coat, his belongings.

In return he was granted a gift from the tribe. The elderly man refused because knowledge was all he sought. For his generosity and kindness, the leader bestowed upon him the gift of the island, the knowledge of magic.

The elderly man grateful for the gift promised to spread the magic to all he came by. He left the island and headed back to his home land. There, he traveled across the land of Thamaturga sharing a small piece of magic with those he met along the way. When all his knowledge was shared, the world became a diverse and exotic place like unto the island that gave him his gift.

Book 1

The Traveler

Chapter 1

Time

Raina

I was eight years old when my world changed. My mother, father, and I were playing outside in the meadow by our home at the edge of the village. I was laying on the grass with a butterfly on my shoulder. Life was peaceful. Then we heard the warning bells call from the village center. Raiders had been spotted attacking surrounding villages. Now, they were coming to ours. The bells rang violently. My mother snatched me up. We all ran to the protection of our home.

Inside, my father grabbed his sword. He stood in the frame of the door. Ready to protect us.

"He is here, I see him at the edge of the meadow. You know what must be done" my father said as he shut the door behind him.

Mother embraced me. "This will hurt little one." I watched as she took a twig from the fire. The end still glowing with red amber. She began chanting. Took the upper part of my arm, turned it toward her and burned into my skin unknown symbols. I screamed in pain. My whole body attacked with a thousand needles. She blew on my arm. The pain left instantly. Then again she began chanting. I shook my head and began screaming.

"No! No mom! Please, No!"

Tears running down my cheeks. She grabbed hold of my thigh and again touched the smoldering twig to my skin. Immediately pain surged through my whole body. She blew on my leg and threw the twig into the fire. Hugged me once more. I could hear the fighting going on outside our door. My mother turned our kitchen table over and we huddled behind it.

The fighting outside stopped. I grabbed my mothers skirt for comfort. She moved her hand in an effort to comfort me, when our door burst open by a demon of a creature, a Raider.

He was large, brownish green in color. Covered in a deep brown leather vest and blood stained pants. The color only highlighted the sickening green of his skin. His shoulders broader than the door frame. He crouched his greasy long black haired head down to walk in. His face was cratered with boils bursting to open. Teeth yellow and jagged. He snarled at my mother. All I could do was hold my mothers skirt and not scream. She began throwing pans, pots, knives, kettles and even logs from the fire at the beastly man. Nothing stopped him from moving towards us. He grabbed her by the throat and lifted her off the floor over the table. He threw her to the floor. Pinning her there with his legs. I was still hiding behind our over turned table unable to move. He pulled his sword and was posed to kill her, when an old man walked into the room.

He was tall with grey long wiry hair tied back in a leather strap. He had a matching wiry beard that stretched to his navel. Unlike the demon man that entered our home, he had pale skin and wore fine velvet robes in red and purple. When I looked at him, a chill ran down my spine.

With a wave of his hand he threw the beast against the far wall of our home, breaking his neck as he did so. I watched the old man. A milky silver snake made of air moved from behind him. It coiled effortlessly around my mother's ankles and wrapped her up to her chin, constricting and gaging her. She was lifted off the floor and was level with his eyes. He spoke to her in a low voice. When he was done, my mother dropped in a heap to the floor. Eyes closed and no longer moving. I stayed frozen where I was. I watched as my mother was wrapped and lifted again to float out of the room behind him.

Then I moved to the frame of the door trying to remain hidden. I saw my father laying on the ground a few paces from our door. He was lying in a pool of blood and unmoving. His eyes wide open. I knew then he was dead. Tears were running down my face. My hands shaking from the shock. I looked around to our neighbors. The bloody paths towards the village center filled with dead bodies of friends and loved ones. I looked back towards my mother. I watched as she was put into a wooden cage cart.

I heard a horn resound through the village. One by one the homes and streets were emptied of the Raiders. They had plundered the homes taking all manner of precious things. They loaded their wagons and gathered in a line. The horn blew again. Together they marched across the meadow toward the Cheyenne path. I waited till they were out of site, then knelt by my fathers side, the tears no longer flowing. I looked around. Yelled for help. No one came. I took in a deep breath. Went into our home, found my satchel. Filled it with a loaf of bread and dried meat. Then headed out on the path to follow my mother. They lead me to this fortress.

That was ten years ago. Now, here I am sitting outside my mother's prison cell bars with my three traveling companions, all watching as she combined herbs and chanted in the language that gave me my scars.

My mother's cell was isolated from all the others. The cells were cold, grey and small. A pile of old hay was tucked into the corner against the stone brick wall. There were no windows and only one entrance into this part of the prison. There were four cells in this wing of the fortress. All empty with the exception of hers. Once in a while, they would bring someone into one of the other cells, but they never stayed for long.

I was happy for her isolation. It allowed me to come as I pleased. No guards were ever posted to her cell. No guards were ever posted to her floor. She was truly alone here. My heart ached knowing I was leaving her. We had discussed me leaving many times. I was never ready. I still wasn't ready. I had lived here in hiding for ten years.

Going out in the world without her scared me. However, now was the time. I felt things were changing I could feel the electricity in the air. My mother new it too, said she could read the signs and insisted we leave the fortress. I knew instinctively she was right, but still I hated to go. I had prepped a bag of scraps. Food, water that I took from the Raiders kitchen for Keiko to carry. I was checking the fastener of the bag that hung over her shoulder.

Keiko was the oldest of the three at Six years. She was slightly taller then the others with curly blondish brown hair, emerald green eyes and a mischievous smile that would make you wonder what trouble she was up to. I had to entrust her to care, protect, and mother them all. It was a huge responsibility for any child, let alone one so young. There was no other option. I too sported a small bag with scraps of food and water. It was flung over my shoulder, and in my waistband two small daggers. It was almost time to go.

Over the past few months the children and I had been sneaking around collecting various ingredients my mother needed for this potion. When I was young, I learned how to travel through the fortress unseen. Moving about was second nature. I could get to any part of the fortress, outside to the woods, or down to the river. In ten years, I had only been seen once.

The potion was now ready for the final ingredient. Looking at me, my mother asked for the fresh bulb of a red thistle flower. This was a rare ugly weed. Long red stalk with talon like thorns. The flower was composed of black petals and a deep purple bulb. My mom wanted the bulb. She knew I could get it. I had seen it in Nezra's quarters. I hated to go there. He was the cruel old man who stole my mother from me.

With the memories of my childhood fresh in my mind, a chill ran down my spine. I traveled the length of the fortress. I slipped through the crack in the stone that would put me behind a tapestry in Nezra's library. I had to go deeper into his quarters, to the garden, to get the bulb. It was three rooms in. So cautiously I crept, staying light on my feet, keeping to the shadows and staying hidden in the tapestries. I went past the tapestry of the map that I had spent hours studying, knew it by heart. I had recalled it for my mother, together we made a travel plan to safety. The town we were headed to was secret, not on the map. It would keep us safe. It was protected by rock cliffs surrounding it on three sides, and the sea on the other.

I had made it thru two of the rooms now and could see the entrance to the garden room. I was hidden behind another tapestry that hung from the ceiling to the floor. This one was a picture of Nezra and a women.

I heard heavy footsteps coming my way. I moved into the center of the picture, hiding my form in one of the large creases of the fabric. The footsteps stopped and I could hear the heavy breathing. It was probably a Raider. Nezra didn't breathe that loud. I noticed a small hole in the tapestry a few inches to my side. I slide into a position to look out the tiny opening.

Shifting thru piles of papers and scrolls was a Raider. He snorted and pulled out a scroll of a map similar to the large one hanging on the opposite wall. Only this one had strange markings on the edges of the map. I heard more heavy footsteps. Two more Raiders entered the room.

"Did you find the map?" The first snorted angrily.

"See we've been out there before." The second grunted.

"It's a waste of time, no spoils to bring back. Why does he want us to go back?" The first one questioned.

"You should know your place." The third commanded.

"I know my place do you?" Was the first raiders response!

The fighting between them began. First shoving, then the clashing of swords. I moved quickly to the edge of the tapestry just as one of them swung at the fabric, slicing it down the middle with his thick blade. If I had stayed, I would be dead.

The fighting didn't stop. One now had blood running down his side, but that didn't stop him from rushing the other two. I took the distraction as a chance to run to the garden to hide. I made it around the corner out of view. I peeked my head through the plants to watch the commotion. Then I heard the thunderous voice of Nezra command them to stop. I watched as he entered the room. He slaughtered them all with a wave of his hand. He picked up the map, turned on his heels and left the room. Panic filled me.

With trembling hands I began searching for the flower. It only bloomed once every ten years. We had been waiting patiently for it to be ready. I found it hidden behind two larger thorn covered plants. There was only one flower in full bloom. I didn't care about the scratches or thorns; I just wanted to be out of this part of the fortress. I grabbed the bulb. Ran out of the wing. Jumped over the pile of dead bodies and slid into the hole in the wood floor onto a trellis headed in the direction of my mother.

My heart was still racing, I had made it back to her. I watched as she separate the bulb of the flower and placed it in the bowl, I was glad I wouldn't have to see Nezra again. Silently we all sat watching her, our goodbyes already said, instructions given. My mother mashed the bulb into the mixture. A wisp of green smoke left the bowl. I didn't have the talent she did when it came to potions. Mine would end up as a pile of soupy paste that did nothing. I could speak the same words as her, and still nothing. I was not gifted like she was.

"I still think you should send me first. Then I will be waiting for them." I said.

"There is not enough here to send us all." She expressed with a concerned look on her face. "If I send them first, they will be together. If I send you first and the potion is not enough, then what? How will you find them? Do I let Keiko be all alone, or maybe Juji or Wyatt? Maybe leave one here trapped with me. Who would you leave to fend for themselves? This is better! Together they are better! You will find them."

I knew my mother was right. The children had a better chance of watching over each other together then separated. That didn't stop me from worrying.

My mother was looking at Keiko. Waving her hand over the bowl. The potion was working. A ray of light the colors of sunrise shot up in a circle around Keiko. It only took seconds and she was gone. With it, a third of the potion. Juji was next. The same beautiful light of fire encircling her, then Wyatt. Once all three were gone, my mother looked at me. Barely a spoonful of potion left.

"There's not enough to get you to them." She quietly said, "Find them!"

"I'll do my best."

Was all I got to say before she was no longer in my sight, but a flaming haze of light in her place. As quick as it started it ended. I was now standing in a meadow surrounded by wild grass that I was barely taller then. No one in site. A thin remnant of a path in front of me. Panic swelled up inside and I ran.

Chapter 2

Run

Raina

My breath was heavy and my legs felt like lead, but I kept running. My mind glimpsing back to images of the fortress. My mom whispering to me. I knew she would keep me headed in the same direction. I just needed faith that this path would lead me to them.

It had taken me all day and late into the night when I reached a solitary stone building in the midst of an open field. There was no roof and two of four walls were crumbling to the ground. There was no sign of movement. I walked into the center of the structure. My only greeting; piles of more stone fallen years before. I glanced around. My eyes began to swell with tears. My fear of losing them getting the better of me. I sat in the dirt and allowed myself a moment to cry. As I did, the exhaustion from running hit me and I drifted into a tortured sleep.

Morning came, a ray of sunlight hitting my face telling me it was time to wake up. I rubbed my swollen eyes. Looked around. The sun was barely above the horizon. That's when I saw them, the small footprints in the dirt. The finger drawing in the sand. The pile of grass and flowers in the corner. They had been here. My heart leapt with joy. I followed the tracks out the side of the building and to another path. I began running again. Following the tiny sets of footprints. Eager to catch up to my little group.

The sun was now setting, or at least I thought it was, the clouds had turned grey and the sky overcast. A low fog began to stick to the ground. Making it hard to see the path. The trail seemed to be leading to a decaying old town in the distance. It would make sense they would continue toward it and find shelter for the night. My anxiety was bubbling up. I hoped they would be there, that I had finally caught up to them.

As I entered the town, something seemed off. The hairs on the back of my neck stood up. My nerves were on edge. I gingerly walked down the middle of the single street. I could no longer see the ground, or for that matter distinguish any tracks without the sun or moonlight. They had to of continued this way, I thought. I kept an eye out for them as I walked. A night chill had set in. The moon stayed hidden behind the clouds. The homes and buildings here were made of weathered wood stacked together as if needing each other for support. The smell of decay and rot hung in the air. If I hadn't been used to the smell I would have vomited. The windows were cracked and broken with torn battered curtains swaying in the light breeze. You could hear the wood creaking as if it was warning you of danger ahead.

I had seen many things, but this, it sent a warning chill up my spine. Fear for the children started to take over my mind. I turned down the only other street in this forgotten town. As

I rounded the corner there were people sitting on the ground, leaning against the walls, standing still in place stopped for no reason at all. I froze. I crouched down moving into the shadows, getting ready to defend myself. I looked closely to see if I could identify the three familiar faces of my group hiding amongst the crowd.

All I found were hunched over, drab lifeless people. They had no color in their faces. Worn, torn clothing hung loosely on there skeleton thin bodies. Each face hollow from lack of food and sun. If they were a threat, it wouldn't be much of a fight for me. I doubted they had the energy to even lift a finger, let alone fight or chase me. None looked up at me. These people were as weathered as this town was and of no threat.

I looked again at the shadows, no sign of the children. I looked back at the way I had come contemplating back tracking. There, coming out from the fog lifeless people. They looked as if the fog was carrying them into this town. The sound of rusted metal clanked against the night. I turned in a slow circle assessing my situation. Only two streets. The way I had come, or continue on. I could go back and go around this place, through the briars and thicket I had just come, but the tracks had led me this direction, I knew they had passed through if not still here. I decided to continue on. The two small blades I packed in my back waist band came out.

I had gathered these daggers when I was ten from a pile of discarded weapons and clothing back at the fortress.

Normally the Raiders would keep these gems, but they were to small for there large hands. Perfect for me. I had spent years learning to fight with them. Perfecting my stealth and technique. Many prisoners I had helped, would teach and spar with me for trade of food, water, and escape. I was always happy to oblige. I would have provided that anyway, but now I was getting training. Win, win in my mind. I held one in each hand now. I would be ready to defend myself if needed. I then began a slow crouched walk through the street to the edge of the town and the briars beyond. Still looking for my family.

I made it to the end, with no problems. No one moved. No one breathed. No one cared I was there. The children were not there from what I could tell. I could only wonder what was going on there? I needed to find the kids and get moving on as quickly as possible. The path appeared in patches underneath the fog. It took me back into the briars, and thicket.

There were odd shaped crooked trees spread across the land. The trees I passed looked like old men with canes petrified in place, and a chill in my spine manifested. The low fog began to thicken again and clutched the ground. Making the path I was on hard to find. I continued walking through the trees and thicket in the direction the path was originally headed, the tiredness of the night was starting to get to me.

I had been running since sunrise, only stopping long enough to check the tracks on the path I was following. My mind began to fill with a heavy fog of sleep. My focus waning from my task at hand. My legs became so heavy; as if I was dragging large iron chains spiked to the ground. I needed to rest but dared not stop. Fear encircled me. My mind started to drift even more. I began to justify that a few minutes of rest would probably help me be more aware. If I closed my eyes for only a few minutes my search would be faster and my head clearer.

Giving in to reason, I sat on the ground with my back against a bent and twisted old man of a tree. I could feel the discomfort in my back yelling at me in pain and feel the thorns of the bushes surrounding me dig into my skin. My mind was so heavy in that moment that I didn't care. Five Minutes. I only need five minutes I thought.

Sleep came quick, my mind filling with images of torture and pain. I recalled hiding behind the wooden table of my home as I watched my mother taken before my eyes. Images of the dead. My father laying before me. I couldn't wake up from this dream. Every scream of pain I had heard, every crack of the whip, or howl of sorrow from prisoners, all holding my mind captive. Memory after bad memory plaguing me. Each dream pulling at me, making me feel weak and helpless. Then, I saw a woman standing in front of me. "Wake up!" she said. "Wake up!" she repeated authoritatively. My eyes flew open.

My eyes were open, but there was a fog on my mind and haze to my sight. Think, I scolded myself. I was sitting on the path. Think, no, I am not on the path. Where are the crooked trees and briars that poked at me? Where am I? I started to move and as I did my mind fog lifted and my eyes began to focus.

This was a dank dark cave. Lifting my head to see, I looked out over the hills and valleys of the floor. There was a soft red glow stretching in painted patterns across the floor of the cavern. I followed one of the florescent trails, it was like the vine of an ivy circling in patterns over the hills and then up the side of the cavern. It climbed intertwining with other vines toward the center where it wrapped around a dull metal crouched appendage. There were many veins of this dusty light creating patterns on the walls and ceiling. The soft glow giving me enough light to see.

The metal arms I saw hanging from the ceiling were made of dull steel. They were unmoving at the current time. They were long thin metal pieces with two hinges that made it fold into itself like bats tucked asleep. I moved to get up. As I did, I realized I was not alone. There were numerous people laying in this cave. Stacked together like dirty piles of laundry. These were not hills and valleys with in the cavern like I had originally thought, but piles of people. I looked down at my sleeping companions. I tried quietly shaking awake the person next to me, but to no avail. Then tried another and another. Shaking did not work, slapping did not work. I even tried cutting one on the arm to see if the pain would wake them up. It should have, but didn't. I tried everything I could short of screaming. I dared not yell or scream incase I would awaken the owner of the metal appendages that hung from above.

I didn't know this place or how I got here, but the chill down my spine said now was the time to leave. I dusted off the glowing vein that was stretched across my skirt. It blew away like dust in the wind. Then I started hopping over bodies and with effort stepped on as few people as possible. Still none stirred. Only the odd sound of silent screams broke the stillness of the cavern I was in. I searched pile after pile looking for my family. There were no children in site. No children in any of the piles. I took hope that they were not in this place lost in a nightmare.

Exiting the cavern only lead to multiple openings and more tunnels. Each tunnel I ran down ended in another cavern all filled with the same slumbering piles of people and now animals and other such creatures. All with wrenched metal arms hovering above in wait. What is this place? I thought to myself. I looped through one cavern and then another. Hitting a dead end. I back tracked. Turning right this time, then left then left and a right. Nope, try again. It felt like hours. I was getting desperate. The fear overtaking my mind. My body began shaking. I was thinking that I would be trapped in here. Then I saw a dim lit crack. A small wedge of light shining into this otherwise bleak cavern. This had to lead outside, just had to. The desperation gnawing at me now flickered with hope.

I ran toward the crack only to realize it was a reflection. I needed to think. If this was a reflection, then where was the actual hole. I slowly assessed the part of the cavern I was in. It linked to two other caverns. Then I saw it. The metal arm from the ceiling that was reflecting the light. I followed the reflections from one arm to the other. Then it disappeared. I knew which cavern held the original light source and so I ran.

The opening was small, but I could work with that. I had been in tighter jams at the fortress. I knew I would have to backtrack to get to it. To many piles of people in the way. Hope was rising up inside me. This was my way out. I backtracked through another cave to get to the other end of the large cavern that held my escape. I ran to it, not knowing a pair of eyes were now watching me.

Chapter 3

Koboldrone

Leon

I saw the swing of his arm but couldn't duck fast enough catching a portion of his paw as it hit me across my face almost knocked me unconscious. His other claw snagged me across my arm. Blood dripped down my hand to the ground. How many were there? I complained. This was the fifth Asbjorn in a row and they were getting stronger. Why were they attacking my village? I had to ask myself.

This was not their normal behavior. They were territorial beasts. Having this many in a short time I knew something was off. The one I was fighting now was black as night. Fur from head to toe. Sharp poisonous red and purple spines lined his back from his head down to his short fur covered tail and he was standing on edge. His snout covered in saliva that whipped off his purple elongated tongue, and sharp fang like teeth to cover his face with slime. His piercing black eyes followed my every move. Standing over thirteen feet tall and another six feet wide he was a force to be reckoned with.

With a sharp growl he swung and this time I dodged it. The only thing I could do was stay out of its way. I was to tired to fight. I ran behind a tree. I needed to put some obstacles between us. Get a game plan together, save my energy, attack, and kill this beast. My village was at stake. I ran to a large boulder further away and crouched behind it. I needed to get my mind working. Out think the beast. I was so tired. "Boom" the crash of a tree hitting the ground some 50 paces away. Then another sharp roaring growl. I tried to focus, but an unusual smell of summer peeked into my senses. I shook my head clearing it of the smell and trying to think. As quick as it came it was gone and my focus shifted back to the Asbjorn. "Crash" another tree hit the ground closer this time. Then I heard a rock smashing into the boulder I was crouched behind. He would be on top of me soon. My mind filled again with the sweet scent of summer my focus wavering from the beast. My senses were overrun with smells of fresh dew in the morning, meadows of wild flowers in bloom, green grass after a summer rain, all making me feel as if I could do anything, the world was full of hope and possibility. It was the smell of my childhood. I breathed it in and my eyes flew open.

What I saw was not the forest or an Absjorn, but a dark cavern and a whisper of girl run by. She was dressed in black from head to toe. With dirty blonde braids stretching down her back. She had a layered long sleeve shirt that tucked into a black leather belt. I could see a small set of daggers poking out of her waist. She wore a black leather pleated knee length skirt over black shorts. Only her dirty knees poked out. Her legs were clad in long black socks and knee high lace up black boots. She was covered in dirt and dust from head to toe. I dared not move as I watched her. Who was this person, why was she here, I asked myself. As she rounded the corner, her scent began to disappear. I was compelled to follow. Whether I liked it or not, she may have just saved me. It was our tradition to owe a life debt in return. I began pushing beasts off me so I could move. I managed to get out from under them all and went in search of this girl.

My day had not started like this; at least I hoped it was still the same day. I wasn't sure how many days had passed since I began the nightmares. I was out tracking one of those horrifying Asbjorn that had ventured onto our territory. So focused was I on tracking the beast. That I didn't realized where I was until it was to late. The mist of the Koboldrone had taken hold causing a fog of sleep and nightmares to take over my mind. I recalled the feeling of metal against my skin, lifting me up. A light breeze brushing across my face as I floated in my dream like state.

Our elders had warned us of this place. As children we were told stories to scare us in the night. I had seen the results of this place and knew that the stories were true. They told of the bending crooked trees that once were warriors now cursed into twisted pieces of wood. Of the mist that would cover the ground, making you lose your way. The nightmares that would make you mad. Echo's of screams in the air that nobody would hear. Trapped in never ending sleep that magic couldn't break. The metal arms that would come for you. Reaching down to claim the rest of your wake-less life. Extracting of children to be experimented on, cut up, or sacrificed. No one really knew what they did, or how they happened. Rumor was that a great magic created them. A great magic was also the only way to destroy them. Nezra was not even powerful enough to destroy the Koboldrone. Now being here. My childhood nightmares solidified once more, I wondered how true the rest of the rumors were.

I normally stayed clear of this area. However, this time, I had the Asbjorn close in my sights, Wanted it dead so it would not hurt anyone in my village again. Thought I could stay on the edge, finish the job and get out before anything happened. Stupid mistake on my part.

I had found her again. It was easy to pick out her scent. I could see her now and began following her path. She was moving quickly. Light as a feather as she jumped and moved over stacks of silent dyeing creatures. Not afraid of waking them in the least. I knew better then to try. Nothing would arouse them. Our elders had tried many times to wake those that fell in the trap of the Koboldrone.

Wearing sacred rare talismans' to enter such a place and not fall victim themselves. They would carry home the unfortunate. Then try every spell, every potion, every healing our culture new on the sleeping dead. Most would die before the spell was broken. Very few awoke, and even then; their minds were too far gone to ever be themselves again. Living in a trans like state. Death was better for them. The elders of our village soon gave up hope and no longer tried to save the hopeless. Now I wondered how I had awoken, and why did her scent penetrate into the nightmare spell when no one else's did. I needed to know more about this girl. I continued to follow.

Ahead was a small crack in the cave wall with a hint of light dimly shining through. She dug at the opening. Then with a loud pop, I saw one of the arms above her unfold and fall to the ground. It landed inches from her head on top of a pile of the dead. She only stopped for a second then went back to digging at the hole.

When it was wide enough for her to wiggle out she did so with some struggle. Resourceful this girl was. I on the other hand would not be able to do the same. Looking around the room I found a larger rock. Picked it up, headed to the opening. I began swinging at the crack in the wall like a hammer. I wasn't scared I would activate the arms. They had done there task of bringing me here to die. The sound would not bother anyone. Soon I had a good size hole. Pushing away the debris and digging out enough for me to fit, I quickly squeezed through the rock just in time to see her skirt into a long low rusted decaying building. Her scent now gone. I took off running toward the broken glazed glass doors at the front. What kind of trap was I getting myself into now I contemplated.

The building was made of rusted iron and dull grey crumbled clay that matched the stormy sky above. A low hanging roof held up at the corners was sagging like it had held years of water to heavy for it. I was afraid the slightest vibrations would make the whole thing cave in. The glazed glass doors were chipped and broken, I, however, still could not see into the building. There were no other windows, vents, or doors on this sad looking building. I knew it was still part of the Koboldrone. My childhood stories reminding me of the terrors that could await inside. Fear entered my mind.

I slowly opened the door not knowing what I would find. The smell hit me first. Spoiled food, urine, waste, wafted into my nostrils. I tried blowing it out, but the smell was stuck. My head shook in reaction. I was disgusted as the smell now seemed to coat my tongue.

I slowly looked from side to side noting no movement. It was safe for now to step in. There was no one in site. Not even the girl. A few doors to my right, and one to my left. Metal tracks ran the length of the entrance disappearing behind walls and doors. Then, the smell of summer hit me. She was to my right. I took a few steps her direction, and around a giant pile of rotting debris and trash that reached to the ceiling I saw her. It was only for a moment as she slipped into the first door on the right. As it closed I heard the latch of the lock click.

A few steps later I was around the pile of trash tugging on the door. It was locked and would not budge. There was a small window above the handle. I crouched down to look in. I could see a long hall with doors. She was trying all of them. Locked. She kept looking into the low set windows on each. She seemed to be franticly searching for something. Then without warning two metal appendages came from the ceiling pinning her arms to her chest and dragging her into one of the previously locked rooms. She struggled and squirmed to free herself until she was out of my site. I knew then she was in trouble. Considering the look of fear on her face, so did she.

I heard the UN-clicked of the door lock. I pressed it open a little to hard as it slammed against the wall and I ran down the dimly lit channel. Stopping at the door she was forced thru. She was being strapped to one of fifty tables in the room. Arms bound across her chest with one strap. Her legs bound just above the knees with another.

I glanced around the room noticing all the tables were filled with sleeping tranquil children. Each with injected with tubes filled with a stream of red blood stretching across the space of the room. A grey static screen that encompassed the entire wall buzzed at the front filling light into the space. At that moment I feared for her life. I searched for her again near the front. All I could do was watch as a knife came down and sliced her arm just below the shoulder to just above her wrist. Her blood now pooling into a a funnel.

She wasn't watching as her blood siphon through the tubes, or cared that the slow buzzing sound that resounded in the building had sped up. She wasn't concerned that the screen once grey was now red. She was working her way out of the restraints that held her. Managing her escape before a metal tube could pierce her skin. She jumped off the table and ran to the far side of the room and out a side door. My door was still locked. I couldn't follow. I ran to the door I had come from in an attempt to catch her coming from one of the other two doors I had seen.

I ran to the second door. It was locked. No window. The third door was unlocked and extremely heavy to open. It took all my strength to wretch it open. By the time I slipped into the room I was sweating and short of breath.

Inside was a storage room of sorts. Stacks of cloth and shelves filled with clothing. Spoils of the dead I concluded. At the far end another door. I started toward the door, but stopped. She was coming, I could smell her scent getting stronger. I stepped behind it as she swung it open. She came barreling through. She ran to the door I had come from, but it was to heavy for her to move. She turned at that moment and we looked straight at each other. I stepped closer.

A waif of air blew under the door. It was then that the smell of fire hit me. The heavy door behind her swung open at full speed. Hitting her into my arms. Pushing us both out of its path. Not before I heard the smash of bone on metal.

We lay there watching as metal arms raced through the room above us, and out the door she had first come. When the room was clear and the commotion silent, I looked down at this girl I was holding. So vulnerable, fragile. I had a strong urge to hold her, even though we needed to leave.

As soon as the coast was clear she pushed against me. She was gone and running. No, limping as she ran across the hall to the last unchecked door. She swung it open and entered. Gathering myself off the floor I took off after her.

I went to open the door and enter myself, but out she came with three young children in tow. She looked at me with bright blue eyes and a questionable look. All I could do was hold the door open. I myself was baffled by what was going on. Then the first blast shook the building. The smell of fire I had forgotten about, back. Smoke began surrounding the five of us. She picked up the young boy, and I taking cue, grabbed the two remaining children. With unspoken words we ran for the glass doors.

We continued running away from the building. We had only gone half the length when the next explosion quaked the earth making her stumble as she ran. I reached out a hand but she had already steadied herself and we continued to run.

The building exploded again and completely collapsed on itself, then disappeared altogether. My concerns grew. Maybe something in her blood triggered this. Fear captured my mind. Would the explosion signal Nezra to come?

The whole area surrounding us began lifting of mist. Sunshine peeked through the overcast clouds that hovered above. Thistles and briars slowly changing to grass and wild flowers. Trees began to untwist reaching up to the sky. We kept running.

Everything changed. The Koboldrone gone. For now at least. But why? I needed answers to all of my questions. We continued running a little longer, I started turning us north to lead her in the direction of my home lands. We ran for another mile, then she slowed and began to walk.

I slowed my pace to walk beside her. She stopped and put down the young boy she was carrying. I followed suit with the girls I had grabbed. She scooped the unmoving children into a hug and for a few moments I watched as she embraced each of them. She looked at me then and said humbly, "Thank you." Then buried her head back into the children whispering to each.

I was memorized by this display of affection she had for them. My heart reached out to her. I didn't want to take away her hope and tell her that there is nothing we can do for them. I would have our elders try to break this curse, but chances are they would remain in this mindless state forever.

Silently I took a few steps back. I needed to clear my head and assess our situation with my new travel companions. I wondered if it would be safe to bring them home. Would the Elders help them or turn them away? Would I be putting others at risk? Standing here watching her with them. My mind was made up. Taking them home was the right thing to do until a better plan could be made.

Chapter 4

Home

Raina

He looked at me with those brown and gold flecked eyes. They were sad. He just nodded his head at my thanks. I was so happy to be with my family again. I figured we were far enough away to be safe. I felt so relieved, I needed to let my emotions out with a proper hug and kiss for each. As I looked at them. A blank expression was on their little faces. Snap out of it I willed. They were void of all emotion. Same expression as I had found them wearing when they were sitting in that room full of children. All the children had a blank stare on their faces.

The grief began to hit me, all those kids trapped. I didn't have the strength or speed to grab more then my family. I never expected so many of them to be there. Then, for the building to explode! When I ran into that last room and saw them lined against the wall I was overwhelmed. Luckily Keiko, Juji, and Wyatt were sitting together. I pulled them up easily. As I started running, holding on to them tightly, they ran in tote. I yelled at the others to follow, but no one moved. I called to them till we got to the door.

When it swung open without my push I almost dropped Keiko's hand in the panic that had consumed me. I ran thru, determined to get them out. Dragging them behind me. Instead of danger it was that man again. I didn't know why he was there but he seemed to be helping me. Out of the building together we ran. Now here we were, far enough I hoped away from the danger.

I had looked back only once, hoping to see if any of the other children were following. There were none, and I struggled to keep my guilt and grief in check. My only peace was the hope that in their state of mind; they didn't know what had happened. I couldn't dwell on the guilt, so I focused on the hope that I saved my family and they would come back to me.

I kept hugging them, and whispering, it's okay, I love you, we are safe now. Not sure what to do. In return, still, blank eyes stared back at me.

Then, a small hand touched the side of my face. Turning to look at Juji, I could see the recognition and light returning to her eyes. She was the middle child of the three at five years old. Sporting choppy short brown hair and golden brown eyes. Her cheeks rosy, a little chubby, and so kind. The most affectionate and loving of the three. As I looked at her I could see she was scared and happy all at once.

Keiko was next to have the mist remove from her mind. She leaned in and held me around my neck. Tears began flowing down our cheeks. Then I felt the tug of my shirt sleeve. Wyatt was watching me ready for his turn to be hugged. He was the youngest of the group at four and a half years old. He had short blonde hair with a callous in the front, making his hair always stand on edge. Which fit his personality perfectly. He still had a bit of baby fat to him, and was all giggles. The boy was ticklish everywhere.

I pulled him into a hug and together we embraced each other till our fears and doubts were gone. Standing up and looking around the woodlands we were in, I heard Juji ask, "Where are we going?"

"Headed to a new home far from here." Was my reply.

"Where did you go, we waited for you to come?" Keiko chimed in.

"I was looking for you."

"Here we are!" Wyatt giggled out.

At that I tickled his tummy till they were all laughing, putting aside the horrors of the days.

I looked up at my strange companion. He had a shocked look on his face. He was tall in stature. My guess just over six feet tall. He had silky brown hair with highlights of gold running through it. He hadn't shaved in weeks and his scruffy start of a beard had flecks of gold as well. His eyes were a dark brown, very thoughtful, when he didn't look shocked or confused. He carried himself with an air of confidence and wisdom much older then he looked. I guessed he was in his early twenties. Not much older then I am at eighteen. His clothes were plain. Button down long sleeve shirt with small tears. It looked like he had been in a few fights. He was well toned from what I could tell, not to muscly, definitely not weak. He was watching us. I could feel my cheeks heat up so I quickly focused back on the giggling threesome at my feet.

"Time to get moving"

"Do we have to?" I heard in unison.

"Yes, it is time. Who would like to lead the way?"

"Me, pick me, please, pick me, I'm first." Juji was jumping up and down excitedly.

"OK, OK, I pick you."

"We need to keep our eyes out for others that may be on our path. If you see someone, then we must hide." The stranger spoke.

"You mean hide and seek like we always play" Keiko interrupted.

"Yes, we are hiding from anyone we see, but we must hide together. Got it?"

"OK." Then more jiggles from the children.

This was a favorite game, they knew it was a requirement of our safety, but we always pretended it was a game anyway. This simple act saved our hides more than once in the fortress.

We started to walk again, not really knowing where we were headed. This wasn't the direction my mother and I had planned out. The sun was in the wrong placement for us to be headed west. Our guide was steering us another way. My hope was that he would help us, not trap or betray us. If I had to fight him for our freedom, I would. We walked maybe ten meters, when Wyatt was already asking to be carried because his 'legs didn't work anymore.'

As much as my ankle hurt, I couldn't say no. So up he went onto my back. It was easier for me to deal with the pain, and help him out than to carry him in my arms.

No sooner then five minutes had passed and both Keiko and Juji were complaining that there 'legs no longer worked' too. Exhausted and in pain, I was contemplating who's turn would be next, as well as, how I could encourage them to walk, when my dark haired companion lifted Juji onto his shoulder, then reached for Keiko and did the same.

We walked in silence for a while, letting my companion lead us. My mind contemplating all the questions I had for him and which I should ask first.

I settled on, "My name is Raina. This is Keiko, Juji and Wyatt. Thank you for all your help."

He smiled in return, or was it a slight laugh, either way it looked nice on him.

"My name is Leon. I live a couple days walk from here. I thought it would be safest for us to head that direction. Get you food and water before you traveled on." He said with a curious glance up at the two girls make a birds nest out of his hair.

"I appreciate your added help. We all do."

"Who are these guys?" he asked.

That was easy to answer and the question was probably sparked by the fact that Keiko and Juji were now decorating his head with anything within arms reach. Berries, leaves, twigs. I even think I saw a caterpillar, but I wasn't going to tell him. Instead I silently laughed.

"They are my family. Brother and sisters of sorts." I continued, "My mom had come across some women that had been imprisoned while pregnant. She helped see them to give birth and together we hid the children and cared for them. Keiko's mom died 3 years ago. She got sick and couldn't recover with the medicine we had. Juji's mom was sent to the arena a year after Juji was born. She never returned. Wyatt's mom died giving birth. I do not know about their fathers. Fighting the Raiders or possibly dead, who knows. I will search for them when I have the chance. Right now they don't have anyone else, so we adopted them into our family." I paused for a moment considering if I should take a direct approach in my questions with him.

"What are your intentions with us?" I countered a question.

I think I caught him off guard, because he choked on his own air and sputtered a moment. He wasn't use to such direct questions I ventured. Living in the fortress compelled me to be direct. It was the only way I could help others at times.

Leon claimed he had no plans or motives for us, just saw we needed help and thought he would be of assistance. He was traveling home anyway. Why not together. I thought that an honest answer. Before I could ask more, his asked another question.

"How did you keep from falling into the Koboldrone's spell?" Leon inquired.

What was he talking about? I had never heard of the Koboldrone? I think I was looking at him dumbfounded, because he repeated the question and added, "the cave, the building, the town," to the end of his sentence this time.

"Oh, um, I don't know, I was dreaming when a women appeared and told me to wake up, and I did. Then I started searching again for these guys so we could get back to our travels. Were you there at the Koboldrone?"

He hesitated before answering, which made me a bit nervous, then said, "Yes, I was also awakened from my slumber in the cave, and saw you. So, I followed you out and thought I would make sure you were safe. I saw you run into that building. Well, after that here we are."

More questions filled my mind. I felt he knew more and wasn't telling me everything, but then I wasn't sharing with him that we lived in the fortress, or the magic we used to get here. Also, the fact we were hiding from the Raiders, and Nezra. Ooh, that evil man unnerved me even now, so far away. I was truly lucky he didn't know we were living at the fortress. Back on track, my turn I thought.

"What do you do when you're not following people out of caves or causing building to explode and disappear?" I said with a smirk.

He gave a dry laugh and tried shaking off the crown of leaves from his head. He only accomplished dropping the caterpillar down his shirt. By the expression on his face he was not at all happy. The girls were off his shoulders in a flash. He then ripped off his shirt and began whipping it against his back to get it off.

I started laughing so hard I almost tripped on the fallen tree trunk in front of me. I set Wyatt on the ground, walked over, put my hand on his shoulder and gently removed the infestation of the single caterpillar.

Someone this ridiculous about a bug was definitely not going to harm us. If he did lead us into a trap, I was sure that with a single caterpillar I could get us out. With that I let my worries and mind relax.

Chapter 5
Change
Leon

I hate caterpillars! They make me itch. I'm not scared of them, I just hate their itchy sap covered legs sticking to my back. I would have gotten it off to, but the dang thing was in the center of my shoulder blades. No matter how I reached or swatted at it, I couldn't get to it. That's when I heard all the laughing. It just made me mad. Maybe I was mad because I was embarrassed. She put her hand on my shoulder, it was soft to the touch. Displacing my anger for the moment. Gently she removed the caterpillar and set it free. I would have smothered it personally. I hate the things.

Once I got ahold of myself I was able to enjoy the laughing at my expense and joined in. Maybe that's how they handled stress and worry; with a laugh. Not the way I would do it, but I am not them.

I slipped on my shirt and began buttoning it up. I could still feel the soft touch of her hand were it had laid. She was still snickering at me by the time I finished. The sun was low in the sky and I knew night was coming soon. We needed to set up camp and rest. Find food and water, and protect ourselves from anything else that might begin lurking in the dark. At that, I announced we stop for the night.

All I got in return was a sarcastic lift of her eyebrow. "Guess we should" was all she said. Right then all the laughing and fun disappeared. She set to work getting the kids to gather small sticks and branches. They were efficient in their tasks. I couldn't help get the feeling forging for food and warmth was something they did often. It made me sad. I decided to leave them to it and went in search of larger logs for shelter, food, water and something to defend us if needed. I was secretly hoping it would be a quiet night.

Some distance from where we stopped; I found a few trees with three large bushy branches that would work well to provide some shelter from any rain, and hide us from passer by's. I went to work kicking and jumping on the branches to rip them from the trees. I stacked them in a pile and continued looking for something to use as a weapon.

I eventually found a broken branch with a tapered edge. It wasn't the sharpest of points, but would work with enough force to make anything think twice before attacking again. It would have to do. I heard the faint sound of water deeper into the woods. I headed in the direction of the sound.

Soon I came across a peaceful brook. There was green lush vegetation lining the edges of the water. Large leaf banana palm plants, multiple herbs, and cattails. I knelt down at the edge of the brook, gulping in the refreshing cool taste. I took advantage of the water and splashed myself down. Ridding my face and body of sweat and dust. The cool water hydrating my skin and renewing my energy. Guilt from my pleasure crept into my mind. I needed to take some back to the others. Grabbing a banana palm I folded it into a cone and filled it with the refreshing liquid. I took one last drink in the brook myself, stood, then turned to head back.

I already felt like I had been gone for to long. Hurrying to my pile of odd shaped branches, I loaded up and headed back following my tracks to where I had left them for the night.

As I rounded a tree they came into view. I wasn't expecting the sight I saw. So serene it was. A small but effective fire was started. A squirrel was tied to a stick over the fire and sending a smell that made my mouth water and stomach ache. How long had it been since I had eaten? The girls were gathering berries at a nearby bush. However, they had more on their faces and in their mouths then they had gathered onto the leaves for the group. She was sitting next to the fire Wyatt in her lap. Talking and giggling. She was helping him hold a stick in one hand and in the other, one of her small dagger. Together they sharpened the stick to a point. She then leaned in close to his ear and whispered to him alone. A smile from ear to ear appeared on his face. He jumped up and ran to join the girls eating berries. I longed to belong to this family.

I dragged my contribution of branches to the camp, with it, made a heap of noise. She turned to look at the commotion. Worry on her face. It quickly turned to a smile as she looked at me and shook her head. I think I even heard a small laugh. It was then that I saw the small lean to behind her. Nestled in the trees for protection. It was just big enough for the children to lay in. My mind was attacked with more questions. She was either really good at this, or I had been gone longer then I thought. I leaned toward the second.

She waved me over and with a smile. Took the water, giving it to the children to drink first. Then requested me to use the branches to hide the lean to and provide more camouflage and protection for the children. How could I refuse? I put my large branches around the small camp making it disappear. This entitled me to a pat on the back, which I gave myself.

Now that camp was done, I sat on the ground by the fire and took in my surroundings in detail.

The lean to was secure on an 'A' frame of wooden sticks, with plenty of leaves and small branches helping with the disguise. The padding they had put in the shelter was thin but effective adding a bit of warmth and comfort from not being directly on the ground. I looked at Raina, she was covered in dirt and smut except for the fresh leaves wrapped around her arm and ankle. Her boot off to the side, but close enough to grab and run if needed. Everything was in arms length. Small and compact. No one seemed to mind, but me. At six feet, space was nice. I also new that given our situation it was a luxury right now and I probably wouldn't sleep much anyway.

"How is your ankle?" I asked, upset with myself that I had forgotten she had been hurt and cut up. I respected that she didn't complain or fret over her injuries, but looking at the dried blood on her shirt sleeve and bloody foot, I knew it had to be causing her pain.

My thoughts were interrupted by her voice.

"It will be fine, just needed to let the blood pooling under my skin out. I feel better now."

Blood pooling? I have had some internal injuries before, and they always hurt more than if I had just broken or sprained my limbs instead. I reached for her leg and she pulled back.

Not what I was going for. I was working on getting her trust. This action did not show trust. "I only want to help" I said. "There is a creek not far from here. I noticed some herbs that could help the healing process."

At my explanation, she move her leg toward me, and I snatched up her ankle before she could change her mind.

I unwrapped the leaves slowly, as I did, three pairs of eyes were peering over my shoulders.

"You okay Raina?"

"Owwey!"

"Oh my!"

Slipped into my ears from my three little guests. Before I could tell them to get, Raina asked them all for a hug and announced dinner was ready.

Three stomping feet ran around the camp then eventually to her. She was tackled with hugs, kisses and laughter. She then began dishing up the food while I inspected her wound.

The bone wasn't broken, but the muscles were bruised deeply, causing the bleeding and swelling. She was smart to slit her skin and let the blood release. Not something most people would do to themselves. The fact she was still walking and carrying the kids on it, worried me. Ideally she needed to stay off it for a week or so, let it heal. That, unfortunately, was not an option. Until they were at my home, they were still in danger. I set her foot down more gently then I had originally picked it up. She wrapped new leaves on it and tucked it under her skirt so the kids couldn't see it. I ate the small meal quickly. Maybe to quick, cause she gave me that look and half laugh again. My stomach was still aching with hunger. I just needed to remember we are only a day or so from my home and a large banquet of food would await me there.

I asked to look at her arm then. She put her leaf of food down and pushed up her dirty blood stained sleeve. The cut was deeper then I thought. Near her elbow it went all the way to the bone. She was going to need medicine if she didn't want to get an infection. I think she new that.

I thought it best to excuse myself and head to the creek, grab more water for us all, and check the herbs I saw earlier to see if they would in deed be of any help to her arm and ankle. The sooner we got her medicine and help, the better chance of her not getting an infection or fever. Those kids needed her. I didn't want to admit it, but I liked her around to.

Chapter 6
Woods
Raina

Thank goodness he was gone. My skin prickled at his touch. I couldn't feel the pain of my leg or arm. My leg had gone numb hours ago, and I didn't pay my arm any attention. Once when I was running from a raider who spotted me in the fortress, I had to squeeze through a small broken iron opening in one of the cells. It speared me as I went through leaving a cut on my thigh the length of my arm and two knuckles deep. I was lucky it hadn't nicked anything important and that I didn't bleed to death then. I was able to sew my leg shut and using herbs and a potion my mother and the kids put together, stayed the infection. For days I was unable to do much. Keiko had to help take care of me and keep watch over the younger ones.

My mom was so worried. I didn't come to see her for a few weeks. We had never been apart that long, and she aged in her worry for me and the kids. Normally, I could work through the pain and healing process, but this one got the better of me. That's when I started teaching Keiko, Juji, and Wyatt how to care for themselves.

My thoughts were interrupted by Juji, "Sing" and we began singing. It was an old lullaby my mom had sung to me.

It was also the only song we knew. I wasn't very good, but they never minded the tone deaf singing.

Soon all three were sleeping. With the sun down, food in their bellies and the warmth of the fire it was good for them to sleep.

Leon hadn't returned yet. I slipped my sock on and laced up my leather boot gently around my damaged ankle. I stood and looked about. I wanted to check out the area around the outer part of our camp.

There was some elm trees and dogbane behind a bank of pine trees. I knew I could make some cordage with these raw materials. If I had rope, then I could weave a bag for berries and maybe make a small sled so the kids could sit or lay and be dragged to our destination. That should eliminate some pressure off my leg from carrying them. I would collect that on my way back I reminded myself.

I continued further from camp, always keeping the light of the fire within view. No other tracks besides ours. No scat or proof that any animals or people had been by here. My mind was at ease. I cleaned my tracks as I headed back toward the camp grabbing elm bark and dogbane along the way.

I must have fallen asleep mid wrap, because there was a hand on my shoulder nudging me softly awake. My eyes opened and I could see Leon holding the leaf full of water. He offered me a drink. I sat all the way up and drank. It tasted so refreshing. Setting it down, I saw the mashed pulp of herbs ready for application to my skin.

He picked up my leg that was stretched out by the fire and began to unlace my boot. He was halfway down my calf when we heard a low long howl from a wolf some distance away.

Slowly I reached for my daggers. Leon was on his feet and moving out of the camp in the direction of the howl. The low howl echoed again. This time closer. I could hear Leon run deeper into the woods. I then heard a low pitched whistle come from his direction. After that, there was one short howl as if in reply and silence entered the camp.

A few minutes went by before I heard footsteps. With daggers ready, I waited. Leon entered back into our campsite and reset the branches, creating our little protection bubble. I just looked at him, daggers still in hand and a questionable look on my face.

"Just a wolf, and too far away to bother us." Was all he said.

Interesting. My mind trying to connect the dots. Slowly I put my daggers away, but I knew I would sleep with one eye open tonight.

He sat back in front of me reaching for my leg, but I pulled it back and began unlacing my boot the rest of the way. He handed me the paste and I applied it to my leg. Then wrapped it with fresh leaves returned my dirty sock and gingerly re-laced my boot. Then I pushed my sleeves up and began the same process on my arm. I got the paste on all right, but the leaves were giving me trouble. He stopped me then and took over.

He was so close, holding my arm. Face only inches away. It felt safe to be in his hands. He was quick with his work and gentle to my wounds. I was memorized just watching him. He reached up to pull my sleeve back down when our eyes locked. Before I could think, he was kissing me. It was a soft sweet kiss at first. Then the heat swelled up inside me and the kiss deepened. I didn't want it to end. He was first to pull away. I swayed a moment. His movement to pull my sleeve down steadied me. My cheeks burned with heat. My heart raced. I could only look down at the ground.

I decided it best to occupy my mind with something else. So, I looked at the cord I had started earlier. I had about six feet. I figure another two and we should be good to go in the morning. I waited patiently for him to move, and when he did the cold chill that took his place was depressing and disappointing at best. He shifted his position to sit across from me, picked up the rope and started helping me in silence.

The silence was exasperating. I thought I would get us talking again.

"You never said what you do."

"I help protect and guard my village." Was all he said.

"Would they welcome us passing through?"

"No, I will have to seek permission for you to enter passage through our village from our Council."

"Did you know that wolf that howled?"

If I wasn't paying attention I would have missed the surprise that ran across his face. He composed himself quickly and looked at me thoughtfully, as if he was determining what the best answer would be.

Finally he replied, "Yes."

"Will he or others like him hurt the children and me?"

"No," he said shaking his head. Realizing he needed to explain now that the wolf was out of the bag.

"He was out searching for me. I have been gone a while, due to the Koboldrone. He has gone back to tell the others I am alive and headed back."

"Does he know we are with you?"

"No, I will ask the Council myself when it is time. We are still a day and a half away from my village. What are we making?" Suddenly interested in the rope. Eyes fixed on what my hands were doing. I decided to give him a break from my questions. Tomorrow was a new day.

"I am making cord. I want to tie sticks together and make a cart to pull the kids tomorrow."

"I can help with that." Was his reply.

I picked out some strips of bark and showed him from across the fire how to twist them together to make stronger cord. I didn't think my nerves could handle touching his hands, or sitting so close to him. For the next hour or so we worked in silence till all the supplies I had gathered were gone.

I was tired. I set the rope to the side, curled up next to Juji at the edge of the lean to and laid down. My bad arm wrapping around the kids, my good one under my head. It didn't take long for sleep to come. It was a light sleep. I could hear Leon stoke the fire. He was moving around. Probably couldn't sleep. He began to move further and further away from the camp. When he was some distance away I heard a low long whistle. It was similar to the one earlier in the evening. A soft howl replied back. The dots were connecting then. Leon had called back the wolf. Some time later I heard men talking. I was drifting in and out of sleep, my mind playing tricks. The rumble of their voices encouraging me to sleep. Soon, I heard no more.

Chapter 7
Chief
Leon

I couldn't sleep last night. The softness of her skin still resinated on my fingers. The feel of her lips still resting on mine. Her aroma intoxicating at such close quarters. I don't know why I kissed her. When I looked into her eyes, my instincts took over. I have never experienced an urge so powerful before. I must still have some Koboldrone curse enhancing my emotions and urges. The only other explanation to enter my mind was she could be my true mate. The Koboldrone was a more logical explanation. I could tell she was not of our kind. So my urges for her could not be the mating call.

I just couldn't wrap my head around it. I tried laying down but ended up tossing and turning for a while. I decided to scout out ahead on the trail. First I stoked the fire, the smoke masking the groups scent. Then I pushed in the branches to hide the light of the flame. I took off in the direction we would travel come morning.

I was far enough away from camp that her scent was gone. I needed to talk with my people. I gave a low long whistle. Waited. Then whistled again. Not much later a howl echoed my call. I ran in the direction of the sound.

There I met up with the wolf. It was my brother in law Ethan. He was older then me by a few years. Hair black as night, eyes silver as the moon. We were about the same height and stature. He was good for my sister. To me, like a brother. At seeing one another we embraced.

"Where have you been? Man you smell! It's been over a week since you went chasing that Asbjorn, not to mention making the Elders Council nervous with your absence and then there's Sanna. She has been hounding me daily to find you. We've got territory disputes happening to the South, rogue wolf packs to the North, not to mention the upcoming nuptials you are supposed to be hosting. Everyone has been asking." Ethan sounded very upset that I had been gone but eyed me with a mischievous grin. "Is that a hint of a women I smell on you?"

I couldn't get a word in edgewise. When I finally did, I blurted out my answer a little to hastily.

"Long story, got caught by the Koboldrone."

His brows peaked. Lips pressed to a frown. Before he could say anything more I made my wishes known. I didn't want to spend time answering questions.

"Brother, don't ask about the Koboldrone, I will tell you later. I will be a day and a half behind you. I need a Council with the Elders please arrange this upon my arrival. If I need additional help, I will reach out to you. In the meantime, I have some duties to attend to and wish no company."

As chieftain of my village I was afforded certain privileges. Of which included giving orders and not being questioned. Tonight, I took advantage of that privilege. With that I gave one last embrace and sent him on his way. He gave me a mischievous smile then took off toward the village. I headed back to the hidden camp. Then headed east scouting for any signs of being followed and started covering up the trail we had made the day before. When I was satisfied that we were safe, I headed to the river to collect more herbs. Dawn was starting to break over the horizon. We would be traveling soon.

Chapter 8

Morning
Raina

Morning came quickly. The sun's warmth hitting my cheek and piercing my eyes when it broke the horizon. It was a matter of time before the little ones would wake. Carefully I slipped out of Juji's grip and sat up.

Thinking back on the night, I remembered hearing him walk into camp, the sound of the fire being put out. The soft sound of his breathing sometime early in the morning hours. Now, looking around the camp, he was already up and gone again.

I carefully put weight on my ankle. It felt better. No longer was I plagued with sharp pains shooting up my leg, or numbness, just a constant dull annoying pain and stinging around the slit I had made. I noticed the fresh paste and leaves sitting by the ashes and went to work prepping my ankle and arm. When I finished, I decided to grab some berries and nuts for the kids and our travels. They would be hungry when they awoke. I was glad they had all slept soundly through the night.

I went out of the encampment as quietly as I could. I didn't want to venture far, incase one of them awoke, also if danger came by. I wanted to be within earshot or have a visual.

The bushes immediately around the camp were barren. Probably from our gathering the night before. I moved a tad further out where I could see some berry bushes full and ripe for the picking. Quietly I went to work collecting. These would make a nice meal. The bush in front of me began to move. I waited patiently, soon the large jackrabbit nibbled its way out of the bush and crossed my path.

A smile lifted my face. Breakfast.

Chapter 9
Asbjorn
Leon

    I wasn't far from my second trip back to camp. The sun had been up a few hours now. They would be waking soon. I walked slowly still wrestling with the events from the other day in my mind. When I caught that wonderful summer day scent.

    I stopped where I was and looked toward the direction of the aroma. It was south of the camp. No more then a few trees from me I saw her. She was slowly moving toward a bush, dagger in hand. With graceful stealth, snatched up a hare, slit its throat, and mumbled a few words. She then moved swiftly to an adjacent rock, skinned, gutted and buried the entrails of the hare. Took the meat and skin and headed back to the camp. All while I stood there with my mouth gaping open.

    More questions built up in my mind. I would have to ask where she learned her skills. They were impressive. I knew very few men that could do what she did that fast. None of them were as quiet and graceful as she was.

    I waited for her to get back to camp before I moved. I didn't want her to know I had been watching her.

When I got back, the fire was going and rabbit cooking. It smelled great and my stomach responded. Lack of food, made me weak. This would be a welcome treat.

She was strapping together the wooden sled that we could pull the children on. I was grateful for the idea, it would save me the embarrassment of another caterpillar incident.

I set the water down and started taking down camp. I wanted no traces we were there. I didn't see anything or anyone the night before, and didn't want to take any chances.

Before I knew it, three giggling children were running around, eating food, and laughing at who knows what. They were such happy kids. Miracle considering. They all took turns running around me, through my legs, and once in a while, grabbing hold of my leg so I could drag them across the ground. Strange, but the events of the morning brought me peace. Normally, I would be annoyed and eventually find an excuse to leave the area. I must still be affected by the Koboldrone, cause I didn't mind.

With camp dismantled and food in our bellies we set out for my home.

The walk was casual. The silence between us natural. I figured the children were more comfortable with me because they began asking me many questions.

"Why is your hair brown?"

"What is that bird?"

"Why is the bird brown?"

"Why is that tree small?"

"Why are you tall?"

"Why is the bird singing?"

"What is the bird singing about?"

I have never had so many nonsensical questions in my life. It went on for hours. All of them taking turns. The only silence I had was when they began feeling tired and laid on the sled. Even then, half hearted questions still poured out of those tiny mouths.

The children were now asleep for a good half an hour when I decided to try to asking her more questions. I, more curious about her then ever.

"How are your wounds?" I started.

"Slow healing, but fine."

"Where are you headed?"

"To a village in the Northern Coast."

"Do you know how to get there?"

"I'll figure it out, but if you have a map of where we are currently, that would help greatly."

"Where did you learn to hunt?"

"Some people I came across taught me to hunt and gave me tips. Do you know how to hunt?"

I coughed on my saliva appalled that she would ask. Of course I did, had the best teachers in the village. It was my calling and responsibility.

"Yeah, a little." Was my response.

Our conversation if you could call it one, was very guarded. The jovial banter and forthcoming of answers gone from the day before.

We were making good time. We could reach my home by midnight at the pace we were moving. The children were in good spirits and well behaved. Lunch was berries and nuts collected on the way and what she had gathered that morning.

Dinner time was on the horizon. I killed a rabbit this time. We built a fire, cooked it while the children rested. Then cleaned up our area and ate as we walked. We still had a few hours of sunlight, and she requested we walk a little further before we camped for the night.

We were well into the territory of my village. Following a path I often wandered that would lead to my home. It ventured thru the trees starting at the edge of our land, then through a meadow of wild flowers, then back into the darkness of the forest. Eventually, it would end at my door step.

We came to the meadow that overlooked the South end of the forest. She stopped and we decided to set up camp. I was okay with this. No one from the village usually came this way. The solidarity of the meadow was a place I often went to sort out my thoughts. Based on my instructions to Ethan, no one would be out looking. I would have one more night to contemplate my argument for the Elders Council.

She had just taken off her boot to check her wound, when we heard the crash of trees to the East and the gut wrenching growl I knew to well.

She was on her feet posed for a fight. Blades in hand, facing the direction of the noise. Children huddle behind her. I respected her gumption, but this was not a fight they should be involved with.

Another crash of trees, and a heavy growl echoed in the air. I moved to her side. Seeing the trees sway from the monstrous beasts movements. I turned to her, "Run! Grab the kids and follow the path to the home at the end, you will be safe there. Now RUN!"

She took a step forward, as the trees parted. Pushing Raina aside, I watched as a grey furred Asbjorn 12 feet tall barreled out of the forest and into the meadow. Coming to a halt less than a hundred meters below us.

I stepped in front of them all, and from the corner of my eye saw her grab the kids, throw our things from the sled, put the kids on and run as fast as she could, sled in tow. I picked up the spear laying on the ground from when she dumped the sled contents. I took a running step and launched the spear aiming for the heart. Grabbed a boulder by my foot, secured it in my hand. I then gave a slow high pitched whistle then charged the beast.

Chapter 10

Cabin

Raina

I had made it about a mile, and could still hear the deafening roars, and sounds of the fight. I looked back at the children. Tears running down their little faces and fear in there eyes. Wyatt was holding my boot as if it would protect him. Juji holding the sled so tight her knuckles were a bright white. Keiko held them both. Protecting them. I kept running, following the path as Leon suggested.

We rounded a large boulder and I came to a complete halt. Jumping into our path a large black wolf. He gnashed his teeth and growled. I pulled my daggers and began circling with him. Always keeping the children behind me for protection. My mind was racing. The wolf crouching, ready to pounce. I was ready.

Then the high pitched slow long whistle from Leon sounded again. As fast as we encountered the wolf he turned his snout and ran in Leon's direction. Within seconds two more wolves coming from the same direction as the first burst through the bushes and ran toward the meadow. I hoped they were going to help. My mind conflicted. Go to the cabin or back and help Leon. What if they were not on his side.

One glance at the children made up my mind. On to the house we ran.

By the time we got there, it was well into the night. My foot swollen and bloody. New cuts along the bottom and sides of my foot from running without the protection of my shoe. I was in pain and completely exhausted. The children had fallen asleep not long ago. The fear and long day getting to them.

I left them hidden behind a bush to the right of the home we had come across. Hoping they wouldn't be seen. I wasn't sure what to expect. It was a modest log cabin home. Stone porch with green tin awning stretching from the roof to the edge of the patio. The build was solid, and seemed to blend into the landscape around it. As if the trees tried to protect the cabin with there branches. With a dagger in each hand, I crept to the door and lightly knocked.

My nerves were frazzled just listening, waiting. No movement could be heard inside. I knocked again, this time louder. Waiting patiently, no answer. I twisted the knob to the door, and it opened easily. I opened it wide and left it open. Hesitating before moving, I gathered my self and in I went.

I searched room to room, no one was there. It seemed relatively safe so I hurried back out to fetch the children. One by one, I carried them in and laid them on a bed I found in one of the adjoining rooms. This cabin had two bedrooms, a simple kitchen, a sitting room, and a single bathroom. It was a luxury to have amenities again. Ten years since I had been in a proper home.

Once all the children were nestled in bed, I bolted the door, found a chair, sat by the unlit fireplace, and waited.

I was awaken by the crashing of wood on the patio and pounding on the door. I grabbed my blades and prepared to fight. The knob turned violently. Then the bolt retracted and the door flew open.

It took a minute while the stranger holding Leon and I evaluated one another. I quickly tucked my blades back in there sheath and moved to help carry Leon to the empty room.

This stranger said nothing. I wasn't going to volunteer any information either. We laid him down. I could see multiple claw marks on his chest, arms and legs. He had blood dripping from his hairline and a rather large bite on his shoulder. He was in bad shape and my heart fluttered that I may loose him.

The stranger left the room and returned moments later with bandages, lotion, and gauze. He too was covered in wounds and bleeding. Getting his own blood on the white of the gauze.

Not looking up at the stranger I said, "I can wrap him if you like?"

He grunted a yes and I heard him leave the room and the door close and bolt behind him.

I assessed the supplies our stranger had brought us. Looking at the bandages, medicine, and blood stained gauze. I needed something to clean him up with so I could dress his wounds. They were deep and bloody themselves.

Finding some rags and fresh water in the kitchen, I started with his head. Once cleaned up, it was a small scratch and nothing to worry about. Next I moved to his shoulder. I washed the area. It would need to be sewn back together. I prepped a needle I found in a basket in the sitting area.

I started the task. To my surprise, his tanned flesh began a transformation. Long golden brown hair began thickening and covering every inch I could see of his body, and his face now transformed to the snout of a wolf. Laying on the bed was no longer a man, but a large beautiful golden brown wolf. I shifted in my seat. I had seen this before in some of the prisoners I'd helped. I wasn't surprised by the transformation, but that he didn't tell me. The rest of the dots from the other night connected completely.

The wolf howl, the men talking, the whistles. He was a shifter and this village was a pack. This is why permission was needed to be here. They did not like outsiders. I moved the needle to get a better grip, he shifted with the move and without warning I felt a sharp pain rush thru my shoulder. He had bit me! It wasn't vicious, but it was forceful enough to break the skin causing me to bleed. My wound would have to wait till he was stable and cared for.

He then transformed back into the man I was getting to know. Gingerly I finished the stitches and wrapped his shoulder. It took another hour to dress and clean all his other wounds. I still needed to stitch my arm, and look at my shoulder and ankle.

Leon was sleeping peacefully, and so where the children, but morning would be upon us soon and I needed a few hours sleep if I was going to be of any use tomorrow.

The morning started with giggles and laughter in the bedroom. That's what awoke me. I was glad to start a new day.

I ravaged the pantry and cooler for food. Prepped a filling meal for us and sent the kids exploring through the cabin. I hoped I could get Leon to eat something. He was still sleeping. I entered the room and shut the door. I didn't want the children scared if he were to change again.

He was sweating and restless in his slumber. I checked his bandages and went about changing them. I had finished with no incidents. I dabbed his brow freeing him from the sweat collecting there, and placed my hand on his forehead. He had a slight fever. I cooled his body the best I could. Then tried to rouse him. He weakly opened an eye and mumbled something undecipherable. I managed a few sips of water, and a handful of bites of food before he slipped back into his restless sleep.

I had each of the kids take turns watching over him and cooling him down with wet rags. While one was busy, the others got a bath and their clothing washed. Soon I had three naked kids exploring the cabin and I was nursemaid to our sick host.

It was well into the night when his fever broke. Rest now came natural to him. After a day of multitasking and worry, I was grateful for the change in Leon's status and the children falling asleep.

Sitting in a chair by his bed, I would kept a vigilant watch through the night, in hopes his fever would not return.

Chapter 11

Night
Leon

It was just past dawn when I stirred awake. My body sore and tight. As I shifted, I could feel the pain of my shoulder shoot thru my body. Then the tightness of bandages wrapping my chest and legs. I blinked rapidly removing the sleep from my mind. I could feel the gentle touch of a hand on my chest, and smell the aroma of summer I had become so accustomed to.

I turned my head and saw Raina sitting on a chair pulled to the side of my bed, hand reached out to me, resting on my chest; foot wrapped and resting on another chair. My heart leaped out to her. She looked so peaceful. She had since showered, and the dirty blonde hair was now flowing down her back like rays of sunshine. Her skin, pale and soft, no longer blood stained and grey from dirt and soot. Her arm bandaged from high on her shoulder to her wrist. Ankle, wrapped and no longer bleeding. I noticed many cuts that were beginning to heal on the bottom of her foot. These were new. I didn't recall her having them at our camp. Then it dawned on me, the meadow, she was not fully dressed.

I didn't want to wake her. I slipped out from the other side of the bed. Slowly I crept through my house. Three clean snuggling babes were in bed in my other room. A line of clothes hung out to dry. Opening the cooler, I saw a plate of food and my stomach growled. Hunger hitting me like a lead boot. I leaned against the pantry and devoured the food. Scrounged around for more and ate till my hunger was no more.

I moved to the washroom and began the process of changing my bandages and applying a special healing lotion our elders make. It would make the wounds heal faster. As I reached my shoulder, pain was moving up and down my arm. With the bandages off, I could see her handy work of stitches. I applied the lotion and the pain instantly subsided. As I finished with the wrap I heard the footsteps of one of my tiny visitors.

Poking my head out of the room, I saw Juji's behind sticking out of the pantry, then slowly start moving up the shelves. She was climbing them.

I walked swiftly over and grabbed her. Giggling, she had two cookies in her hands and proceeded to shove them into her mouth as quickly as possible. I couldn't help but laugh at the sight. She then jumped out of my arms and ran back into the bed she had come from. Within minutes she was quietly breathing and back to sleep.

I needed to see the Elders. I changed my torn up pants and put on a fresh clean shirt. Cautious still not to wake Raina. Out of the cabin I slipped headed to the Council's chambers.

Chapter 12
Sanna
Raina

I awoke stiff with a sore neck, kinked back and ankle throbbing. I looked at the bed. Surprise hit me, Leon was not there. I slowly rubbed the back of my neck and stood. Blood rushed to my ankle and the throbbing worsened. Gently I walked into the main room where I found Keiko and Wyatt playing quietly stacking blocks and wood. Juji was still sleeping.

I searched for something we could eat and settled on cooked oats. As breakfast was about ready I heard an enthusiastic knock on the door.

I wasn't sure if I should answer it, but Wyatt had ran to the door and was already turning the knob to let in our unknown guest.

Standing at the door was a tall slender women. She had olive skin and her face reminded me of Leon. She had darker brown hair then him flowing mid length down her back and deep violet eyes. The color of twilight. She smiled at Wyatt and opened the door wide. I wasn't sure what to do. I just stood there.

"You must be the reason my brother is so mysterious these days?"

I didn't know what to say. Brother? Was he being mysterious? I wouldn't know.

She looked at Wyatt, patted him on the head and then glanced behind her. She was looking for something.

"Sasha, Get in here! Sasha!" She yelled with a smile.

Before I knew it a small young wolf pup with fire red fur crept around the door hinge and hid behind this women's legs.

The minute Wyatt saw her, he tried to grab her.

"Puppy."

Before you could blink, Keiko, Wyatt, and Juji were cooing the pup out from behind the pair of well toned legs. I didn't even know Juji was awake. At the sound of puppy, her eyes must have popped open and there she was in the mist of the group.

"Where are my manners? I'm Sanna. Leon's big sister. This is Sasha. My husband Ethan told me Leon had guests and I had to see for myself. Hallelujah! Miracles must exist."

Sanna sauntered right over to the fire I was standing in front of and started stirring the oats. Before I knew it, we were all eating and talking over breakfast. Sanna was very open, warm and full of questions. She was casual and easy to talk to. My head was spinning from all the information she was giving me and I was surprised at my forthcoming of information in return.

We had been talking while the kids and Sasha played. I had opened up to her about things I had never told a sole. We talked about my life before the fortress. What the fortress was like. How I followed my mother in the prison wagon to the holding cells. People and creatures I had seen. The arena games. How I left. How the kids came to be family. How we got separated. Day to day life? Finally, How we got to here.

Sanna was just as forthcoming about them. She told me that when Leon was twelve years old there village was in a terrible dispute over the Eastern border. Their father, the chief, had taken a pack of warriors to defend the border from Raiders and River Pixie's. They secured the border and made a treaty with the Pixie's. As they were returning home. A small band of Raiders ambushed them. Many were killed, including their father. Leon became chief of the village then. Their mother was so heartbroken and distraught, she left the village. Said she couldn't stay. To many memories. She visits occasionally. Last time, was when Sasha was born.

"So Sasha, can she shape shift back and forth?" I asked.

"Yes, and No. She doesn't have the ability to control her transformations at this young age. Babies are born like you. When they reach about four, sometimes earlier or later depending on there developmental state. They transform to a puppy like state. They can understand you perfectly. If you are one of us, you can understand them back. Sasha will be like this for a few years, then she will be able to start controlling the transformations. It takes practice."

"So, you can transform as well? Can everyone here transform?" I was intrigued by this revelation.

"Yeah, did Leon tell you nothing?"

"Nope, not a thing. Told me he hunted and helped keep the village safe." I said sarcastically.

"That's Leon, the big talker." She rolled her eyes as she spoke.

"Are you all wolves, and how many are you?"

"Yeah, to the South is another group. We rarely see them. There are some rogue packs that are dangerous. They wander the Western woodland area. We stay clear of those woods if we can."

"Do you not travel much then?"

"No, we stick to our lands. Any outside travel requires permission."

"So how does this Elders Council Leon mentioned work?" I asked next.

"The Council was originally put in place over a hundred years ago to assist the Chief. They are to impart knowledge, counsel solutions, and help implement strategies the Chief has decided are best for the Village. When Leon became chief, he was so young, they took on a more active role. He fights with them now all the time. They make laws and rules without his consent. There is one council member, Sr. High Councilman Raoul, who has been trying to help Leon change things back to the way it was. Elder Erebos, if he has his way, would kick Elder Raoul off the council. Luckily, he doesn't have the power to do that. He has however, taken away Raoul's vote in most matters."

"Is that why we need permission to be here?"

"Yes, they put that rule in two days after my mother left; to protect the borders they say. Leon thinks it's more political. Thinks they didn't want our mother influencing him. Raoul says, it to keep out information from the outside world, then whatever lie the Council comes up with must be truth. No one to say otherwise. That's what Leon tells me anyway. We in turn never leave. That's also why our Mom doesn't see us much. Leon says they are the ones stopping her from returning. I believe it. She had to plead with the Council for three months just to visit us when Sasha was born. Even then she was only granted a weeks visit, unable to return permanently."

"Can the villagers or anyone else do anything to stop the Council?"

"Most are scared they will be banished from the village. Lose what protection they have. So it's hard for them."

"Oh, I see." I now had a better understanding of what life was like for Leon, his sister and this village. To me just a bigger cage then the one I had come from.

"So, what was Leon doing outside your boundaries?" My mind again trying to connect the dots. Where we had met was not on their land, and given what Sanna said about leaving seemed odd he would be out there.

"We had an Asbjorn enter the Eastern side of our territory. He went to help. They chased it out of our land. Leon followed. Ethan was with him for a bit. They had lost the trail. Ethan came back. Leon wanted to search more. Sometimes that man can be so stubborn. You know men. They get an idea in their head and there is no stopping them." Sanna replied.

For hours we talked and confided in each other. We were instantly bonded. I liked having a friend. I looked at the time and noticed it was close to lunch, which must have sent off an internal alarm cause Juji and Keiko started mentioning they were hungry; at that Sanna invited us to eat with her family.

I wrote a note for Leon so he would not worry. Out the door we went.

Sanna's' home wasn't much different then Leon's'. Both clean well kept modest log built cabins that blended into the landscape of pine trees and brush. The inside shared a similar layout only her's was painted inside with vibrant colors of yellow and blue. Not the natural color of the wood like Leon's place.

She quickly put us to work helping prep. She also made each of the kids and Sasha take a bath. What a soapy mess. Nothing like a puppy in a tub full of kids. She gave each one a clean new outfit to wear. I was so touched by the gesture my eyes began to water. Then she turned to me

"Your turn. Shower, clean up, bandages are in the drawer, use the cream in the basket by the sink on your wounds. There are clothes in my closet, so pick out an outfit before you go in to bathe. Lunch will be ready in 15 min; don't take to long."

How could I refuse! Into the bedroom I went shutting the door so no one could see the tears of gratitude run down my cheeks. I slid open the door holding her clothes. She had so many bold color choices. Vibrant reds, deep purples, golden yellows. I had never seen such beautiful clothing options. My wardrobe for ten years was black on black on black. Always dark, so I would blend into the shadows. I ran my fingers along the clothes and stopped at a soft sky blue long sleeve shirt. This was the one for me. I let a smile cross my face.

When I stepped out of the washroom, no more was I wearing battered stained black clothing but bright pastels. If my mother could see me now. As I thought it, my heart sank at the thought of her alone still trapped in the fortress. I had taken no more then two steps into the main room when I was greeted by the tall stranger that had dropped Leon at my door. He had short black hair, that was dark as night. Piercing green eyes the color of the pine trees outside the door. He was slightly taller then Leon, about the same physique. Shoulders just a bit broader. A memory of the black wolf from the trail the night prior entered my mind and I made the connection.

"Well, Ethan, introduce yourself! Are you going to just stare at her like before, or do I need to do all the work." Exasperated she shrugged her shoulders and shook her head. With a wave of her hand, "Raina this is my husband Ethan. Ethan, you already met Raina. Now that introductions are done let's eat." I was glad Sanna was around, she made everything seem normal.

They were a cute affectionate couple. Sanna bossed him around. Ethan would wink, and say, "I love you too!" whenever she gave him an order. It was endearing. Reminded me of my parents once long ago. When supper was over, Sanna put Ethan to the task of finding a map. Together Ethan helped me plan my travels up to the Northern Coast. He was very wise giving me information on the landscape, threats to avoid, where Raiders of Nezra were currently and danger signs to watch for. I found it all very helpful. Sanna even volunteered Ethan to gather us some supplies for our trip and see us safely to the Ladow borders. It was all very thoughtful. Our plan was to prepare tomorrow then leave when the sun came up the following day. I would leave earlier, but they were planning to attend a wedding ceremony. I didn't want to impose more than I was.

Night soon fell, I needed to get the kids back to Leon's before they started drifting off. As I searched the small home for them, it was to late, Sasha and Keiko had snuggled into a bed and were fast asleep. Juji and Wyatt not far behind them. At that, Sanna insisted we stay the night.

We sat by the fire listening to Sanna share the latest village gossip. It felt great to fully relax. I had allowed my mind to wonder to the upcoming travels ahead, no longer paying attention to Sanna's gossip. My attention was drawn back to her when she stated the question, "So it's all settled then."

"What is settled?" I inquired, confused by the statement.

"The wedding, you are coming as our guest. I insist."

"No, no, no. I can't come. I don't want to bring attention to myself, and I am not familiar with your customs. So, No, I can't go." I insisted back. Upset with myself for not paying more attention to her.

"You already agreed and I accepted, so to bad." Sanna reprimanded.

Somehow, I got myself roped into festivities that now I couldn't get out of. I could tell by the tone in her voice, she was not going to let me back out. With that finalized the topic was done.

It was getting late. Ethan began trying to get Sanna to go to bed, when the front door flew open with a bang. Leon charged in red faced and out of breath. He looked angry. "Where have you been? I've been looking all over for you!" he practically screamed.

Before I could say anything, from behind me yelling back was Sanna.

"We left you a note. If you had read it, you too would have been invited over for dinner and conversation. Now, acting like a spoiled child, you are not welcome in my home until you apologize. So... I'm waiting ... and while your at it, the children are asleep so keep you voice down." She scolded him.

He looked from me to her to me to Ethan. Who shrugged his shoulders and gave him a 'sorry I can't help you bud' look. Then Leon turned on his heels and headed for the entrance. With a loud slam of the door, left.

Sanna, gave a fuming sigh, then eyed me with a mischievous smile. She then bid me goodnight. Ethan on the other hand followed her with his tail between his legs into his room and shut the door.

I smiled to myself, not really understanding this brother sister dynamic. I laid down on the floor by the fire happy we were safe, happy we had made a friend, happy we had a plan in place. I was at peace. Sleep came easily.

Chapter 13

Council

Leon

The Council Chamber was still dark. It was a tall majestic building made of carved thick cedar with wooden spirals reaching the sky. The ivy covered outer doors were carved with landscapes of Ladow. I entered the building. The foyer vast and open. The ceiling stretching to the tops of the spirals. At the far end two more giant wooden carved doors in a deep red stain stood closed. Only a faint light breaking out from under the door, showed me a sign that they were meeting.

I awaited patiently running over the debating points in my mind. I ran my hand through my hair again. It was my nervous tick. I sat in a chair in the hall awaiting my time. It wouldn't come fast enough.

The door slowly swung open. Elder Raoul stepped out of the deliberation room and walked toward me. He was a kind older man. He had grey hair that was neatly pulled back into a band. He was clean shaven with a chiseled face. Once a large man, now, he was much thinner and frail.

Years ago he had been captured by a Raider party. Taken to Nezra's' fortress. He didn't talk about it much. I knew from stories that he was there for three years before he escaped. He had been to the arena battles, starved and tortured while there. It was rumored that when he finally escaped, it was because he had help from someone on the inside. He made a trade for his freedom.

There were many speculations on what the trade was. Some said he bartered the life of others in hiding. Others said he gave Nezra special recipes for potions in return for his freedom. Still some say he promised Raiders gold and silver from the village treasury to secure his freedom. I didn't give in to village gossip. His past was his to share. Now, he spent his time amongst the ancient books in the Atheneum Library. Taking on a mentorship role within the council rather than deal with the politics and day to day matters.

Elder Raoul came and sat by me. He put his hand on my knee.

"Be cautious of your speech." He warned.

"Is Erebos creating drama in the council?"

"He is causing unrest if that is your question." Elder Raoul responded wisely. "I think it wisest to leave out details that may cause additional questions to be asked." He continued to say. "I will be waiting in the Atheneum amongst my books when you are done. Please do come see me." He stood and continued his slow walk out the main door onto the village paths. I remained seated now deciphering my thoughts.

Another hour past before the thick doors opened again. Elder Erebos stepped into the corridor and waved me to come. He was the opposite of Elder Raoul in every way. Where Raoul was kind and giving. Erebos was cruel and demeaning. Erebos twisted words, meaning, and information to get his agendas passed. He was an arrogant, pompous politician. In my opinion, power hungry. He was head seat of the council. When Raoul stepped back from head seat, Erebos was quick to strike. I think he had something to do with Raoul stepping back. It was luck that Raoul was still on the board. When I needed him, he had my back. The same could not be said for Erebos. I wasn't sure where Erebos's loyalties lied.

I walked into the deliberation room. The room was set up with a half circle of chairs facing a single podium. Two chairs were empty. Mine and Elder Raoul's. I stood at the podium ready to address the council.

Generalization would be best I thought. "I have come to request permission for refugee's that wish to stay within our village border." I started. Any amount of detail would bring on to many questions. I continued. "It is a small family of children seeking our protection." I waited.

"How many are in this family?" Elder Gregory asked.

"Four."

"Please elaborate." He insisted.

"One older girl, two younger girls, and a small boy, Elder."

Elder Gregory continued, "How did you come across them?"

"Headed back from my chase of the Asbjorn, they were on the path ahead of me." I lied.

Elder Erebos chimed in, "On the chase you were not sanctioned to go, is that correct?"

"Yes, Erebos, I did venture out further then required. I am apologetic for my actions of being over zealous in protecting our village." Was my reply.

"In your zealousness, you left your village unprotected. Do you not realize the possible risks you put the village in?" He asked with a sly smile.

"Yes, I thought the risk of the Asbjorn returning was greater than any new risks on the village. We are at peace with our neighbors, and there have been no sightings of Raider parties headed in our direction. Given the Asbjorn attack, I felt the risk of ending the threat a better decision." I snarled back. My temper was coming to the surface. I was having to fight it down and hold my tongue.

"Do you not believe that the decisions here are for the betterment of the whole village," he scolded.

"Of course I do!" I answered shaking my head in unbelief that he would ask that.

"Then why purposely discard the decision of the council in regards to chasing and retaliating against a beast?" he smiled again as he asked.

"Again, I felt that ridding the village of the beast would keep it from returning and causing more injuries or lives. It was not my intention to discard the suggestions of the council. As chief of this village, I am entitled to make alternative decisions for the well fare of the village." I said thru clenched teeth.

"Now that you have dismissed the council and disregarded our requests you would like us to allow for one of yours. Is this correct?" He snickered.

"I did not dismiss or disregard the council. The two instances are not related. I am requesting we do not abandon these children to the threats of the land, and show compassion in allowing them to stay." I was exasperated. I wanted to throw Erebos thru a window.

Erebos smiled again. "So we are UN-compassionate if we choose to deny your request. Have we not shown compassion for our people?"

"Yes, the council has shown compassion, I am asking we show it again."

"You want the council to change the rules because you broke them, to allow people you met on a path you were not to be on in the first place to stay with us? What do you know of them? They could be spy's for Nezra. Have you verified they are not?" Erebos asked.

I could see the other members of the council where nodding in agreement to the idea Raina and the children were spies. I couldn't tell them the truth. It would only lead to more questions and problems. Erebos had already tainted them. Using words like people instead of children, spies instead of travelers. He had twisted my words to influence the board. I ran my hand thru my hair for the umpteenth time knowing the decision would be no, I had lost.

"No, I cannot verify they are not. As children, I would hope they are not. If they were, maybe we can be impressionable enough to gain their loyalty and make them an asset to our village." I responded knowing I was defeated.

The bell was rung. The debate over. Erebos and the Elders took a moment to cast there votes. Six to two was the vote for denying my request. I was given three days to see them out of our borders. I felt deflated. I watched as the council left the room through a back door. Before Erebos left, he turned to me and asked, "If you tracked the Asbjorn, then why did it return before you did?" He smiled at me, walked out door, and let it close behind him. I ran my hand thru my hair again. I turned and headed out to see Elder Raoul. We needed to talk.

The Atheneum was located half a mile away from the council chambers. Most things in our village had a good half or full mile between them. It helped us to control damages and contain threats. If we had people or buildings closer together, there would be the opportunity for more destruction and injuries. I was glad for the walk. It would help me shed the anger and disappointment I felt before seeing Raoul.

Deep in my thoughts, I was at the door to the Atheneum before I knew it. The building was hidden underground. A green carved door stood framed in the forest. It was carved with all manner of animals, plants, and decorations. It was flanked on either side by a large pine trees that hid the walls to the covered stairwell the door opened up into.

I walked down the iron spiral staircase to the open room. Shelves were lined row by row as far as one could see. Tiny orbs floating above the shelves lighted the room. It was as bright as noon day. The walls were carved stone with decorations, stories, and designs. Village artists would come in and add to the collection from time to time. It was always changing.

I walked by several rows of shelves when I saw Raoul sitting in a chair amongst piles of stacked books. He looked up from the scroll he was studying and waved me over. I came and sat on a stack of old herbology books next to him. He rolled the scroll back up and set it to the side of his chair on the floor.

"So my boy, are you going to tell me of your adventure?" He asked with a glint in his eye. Then waited patiently for me to respond.

"Where do I begin?" I said to myself more than him, and ran my fingers thru my hair trying to figure out where to start.

"Begin at the chase. Did you catch him?" He asked eagerly.

"No, I need your help," I started. "I found myself in the Koboldrone's snare. Lost in the nightmares."

"Are you sure it was them?" His eyebrow raised, concern on his face.

"Yes, I met her there. I mean the children there. I don't know what happened. I was trapped in a nightmare, and the next minute I was following this girl. I can't explain it." I was so confused.

Raoul rubbed his chin and nodded. He was thinking. I waited for him to come to a conclusion. After a while he asked, "Explain to me your dream."

I told him my dream, of the smells that entered my mind, of the girl. I then rambled on about the building, arms, red screen, the explosion. Then about the children.

He sat quietly listening to all I had to say. Rubbing his chin he merely said, "I see."

I didn't see. I didn't understand at all what had happened. "What is it?" I asked him. "What can you tell me?"

Raoul responded, "I must seek my books for answers. This will take me some time. Are you sure the girl is not one of us?"

"Yeah, pretty sure. I can find out today when I see her. Do you think you'll have the answers to my questions in these books?" I queried.

"We will see. Met me tomorrow mid day. We will talk then."

At that I said my good byes and left the building. When I opened the door to the outside it was dark. The entire day had slipped by me. I felt a worry in the back of my mind. I had left Raina and the children alone without so much of a word as to my whereabouts. I began to worry about them. How strange it was that in so little time, they had managed to consume my thoughts.

I hurried to my home as quickly as I could without drawing extra attention to myself. The last thing I needed was rumors spreading thru the village. I got to the house and it was completely dark. As late as the hour was, I thought they may be sleeping and didn't want to wake them. I quietly slipped into the house and let my eyes adjust to the darkness before moving about. Raina was not sleeping in the main room. I went to my second bedroom. No one was there. Then to my room. No one there either. Panic began to well up inside me. I turned on lights and rechecked the entire house. It was empty. I ran outside, then down the path that lead to the meadow. No signs of them in the meadow or beyond. I ran back and searched the woods around my home. Had they left? Had they gotten lost? Where could they be? My mind was panicking. I needed help if I was to find them. Ethan would help. He knew they were here anyway. I knew I could trust him to not say anything and keep our search quiet. I ran to Ethan's home.

When I got there, there was still a light on in the main room. I rushed up the porch and threw the door wide open. Surprise hit me at once. There seated comfortably was Raina. Her eyes wide with surprise. I was so angry that they were here and not waiting for me. I blurted out, "Where have you been."

My sister immediately scolded me. I was being played the fool. Embarrassment rushed to my face. Was there a note? I was to busy worrying that I hadn't noticed. I was angry at Ethan for telling Sanna. I should have known better. Sanna was not one to let things lie. I walked out of their home and slammed the door shut to make my point.

I cooled down by the time I got home. Glad that Raina and the children were safe and taken care of. Glad that they were still here. In the back of my mind I was jealous of my sister for snatching her away from me. Tomorrow was a new day, I would get some answers before seeing Raoul. I would go over first thing in the morning, talk with her until I had to met up with Raoul. Raina and I would be able to spend time together. Then we would have all evening as a family. The thought put a smile on my face. Then I remembered the ceremony and my smile disappeared. I only had the morning.

I would make the best of it I thought. Trying to be positive. I laid down to get some rest.

Chapter 19

Market

Raina

Morning came fast. It was a pleasant night. No nightmares, no fussing, no playing nursemaid. Just a quiet, peaceful night. It would be great when this was a regular occurrence in our lives. My mind drifted to the tasks of the day. Today was going to be busy. I stretched out my legs and arched my back. I felt no pain in my ankle or on my arm. I took the bandage off my ankle. If it wasn't for the faint scar from my knife cut, you would never have know I was injured. I went to the washroom to look at my shoulder. Both the cut on my arm and bite in my shoulder gone. I decided to test the agility and movement so I began flapping my arms and waving it about while jumping and shaking my ankle.

I didn't realize Sanna was watching me until I heard the uncontrollable laughter that attacked me from the main room. My cheeks red, I turned just in time to see water come shooting out of Sanna's nose. We both began laughing.

"It's the lotion. It's a special potion to heal. You should be back to normal." Sanna added between laughs. With a smile on my face we began the day.

We started the day at the village market. There were vendors with every kind of ware available. I looked at Sanna.

"I don't have anything to barter with."

Sanna just laughed. "I know, you have nothing to worry about. This is a gift from us to you." She said with a smile and partial squeeze of her arm around my shoulders.

"Thank you," I said again regretting the fact we had to leave. I enjoyed our brief time together. I was sad to see it end. I didn't want to think about the loss, so I focused on the wonder of the market. Sanna took me first to a clothing cart. Sanna was great at picking out the right sizes to fit the kids. We held them up, hem and hawed, then finally decided. When we had finished we found two durable outfits for each of them.

Next we ventured into a shop with clothing my size. I was overwhelmed. I let Sanna pick out a couple outfits for me. Tried them on. Then off we went. We stopped at the tonics peddler and she got me some healing lotion. I was most excited about this. Other than food, it was something I thought would be of use.

Next we headed to a basket weaver and found two over the shoulder bags. Perfect for our supplies. On to the butcher, where Sanna picked up jerky and dried meats. This would quicken our journey allowing us to eat on the walk. Then last to the farmers cart. There were all manner of fruits and vegetables. Many I had never before seen. Sanna riffled through the selection and filled a bag with a variety. I was grateful she was here to help.

We had wrapped up our shopping. When on the way back we passed a toy vender. Sanna stopped. She picked up a rag doll. It wasn't anything grand. My mind took me back to when I was a girl and had one of my own. The ache in my heart manifested. My mother all alone. My father, dead. I watched as she set it down and picked up a wooden horse and cart. Wyatt would adore that. I didn't say a word. Instead I watched in silence. She had the vendor wrap up the horse and cart, and two dolls. We were lucky to have Sanna as a friend. We were almost out of the hustle of the market when we ran into Ethan.

"Where are the kids?" Sanna asked surprised.

"With my mom." Ethan stated as if we should have known. "I went to the cart maker and had this done for Raina!" He almost shouted excitedly.

Behind him was a wooden cart. He showed us all the features. It had a pull out drawer on the bottom for all three children to sleep on. When it was pushed in, it sat all three or provided enough room for two to lay down. It had a hammock on top sturdy enough for a child to sleep on. The wooden rails moved to straighten the hammock into a cover when the drawer was pulled all the way out. It had baskets hanging from the canopy. A bar in the back to push the cart. A lever in the front to pull with. Ethan even said he tested it. "If the slope isn't two steep, you can all sit in the cart and coast down the hills. Beware of making sharp turns," he chuckled. Holding up a scrapped arm.

He continued saying, "You may find it doesn't take sharp turns to well." At that we all laughed. Then came the piece of resistance; a hidden sleeve were in was a long blade. Ethan was smiling from ear to ear. So proud of his contribution. I had to admit, I was impressed. Sanna patted him on the shoulder and nodded, "You did good."

With our new found cart and all our supplies we were ready to go. Sanna helped me get the cart ready for tomorrow. Blankets were added for comfort and warmth. All our supplies loaded into the wagons and baskets. It had taken all morning and into the afternoon, but we were done. I think we both were confident in moving forward with our travel plans.

Now that we were packed for tomorrow, Sanna and her mother-in-law Ethel took me to get ready for the nights activities. Ethan was sent on errands, and the children were having an afternoon nap. Alone, they explained to me how it worked.

"First dinner. Everyone arrives and the banquet begins. Then the couple will arrive and start the first dance. The orbs of light in the sky will enchant the couple causing their scents to be magnified. This is needed for the couple to imprint their scent onto one another." They told me.

Sanna continued, "We are to watch. Then the Village Leader initiates the ceremony. This is Leon. He will address the crowd instructing them of the sanctity of marriage. He is followed by Elder Raoul who initiates the enchantment that begins the mating test. The female is hidden amongst all the eligible women of the village. (She was quick to point out that included me.) Her mate is blinded by enchantment as well as any male of age that is unmated. They are sent to pick out their mate based solely on scent. When he finds her, they dance. All the other males will choose then and everyone dances. Ethan and I, will be able to dance together here as well. He doesn't go thru the enchantment since we are already mated."

She went on to say. "Once the dance is over the enchantment is broken. The identity of the chosen mate revealed. According to the Elders, this helps those eligible find a mate for courting. At the end of the dance, you can give your locket to your dance partner if you want him to pursue you. The ceremony is then sealed by Elder Raoul. Dancing and more dining take over the rest of the evening. It is always a wonderfully enchanted evening." Sanna said with a dreamy look in her eyes.

Then she squinted her eyes and bent her head low to my ears. I knew a juicy peace of gossip was coming. "Sometimes they pick wrong. When they can't find the right mate, the ceremony ends and he is not allowed to mate again until permission from the council is granted.

"Either way," Ethel chimed in, "it is a great party with a fabulous dress."

I was nervous. I didn't have a dress to wear. I was still convinced this was a bad idea. Sanna said she had everything covered. Sanna began by doing my hair and Ethel worked on her hair. Then I watched as Ethel highlighted Sanna's face with special lotions. They looked at me. "Your next." Both of them began putting lotions and powders on my face. It felt foreign and heavy to me. I looked in the small hand held mirror she had asked me to hold. The face that stared back at me glowed with soft rosy pink cheeks, lips a deep varnish red in color. Eyes dusted in sparkle like the deep blue sea making my eyes a bright vivid blue. My skin looked invitingly soft and subtle to touch. I raised my fingers but was to nervous to touch my own face in fear I would rub it off and ruin the art work she had done. I didn't recognize myself.

Once our hair and faces were done Sanna pulled out a glittering dress to change into. She wore a floor length gown with a square neckline. The sleeves were dark at the shoulders and virtually transparent by they time it reached her wrists. It was tailor made to fit her body perfectly. Molding to every inch of her slender frame. The color was vibrant, of twilight shifting to darkness. It highlighted the deep purple of her eyes. As she moved it looked like the hues of night stretching over her body. Changing from light violet to a deep purple. The locket she wore was the same color as her gown. It to changed colors going light and dark as she moved. Always matching the shade of the dress. She was stunning.

I tried straightening the blue shirt she had given me the other day and was trying my best to press out the wrinkles in my skirt. Sanna looked at the clock on the wall, then began pacing. Ethan wasn't home yet. Before she could wear a hole in the floor, in he came. With him, dark dress robes in one hand and a white box tied with a blue bow in the other. He whistling and howled at Sanna as she walked toward him. Sanna took the box from his hands and walked into the bedroom. Ethel and I followed suit.

She pulled out of the box another floor length gown as beautiful and glittery as her own. It wasn't exactly the same as Sanna's but very similar. This floor length gown flared just above the knees giving the image it was floating on water. The neckline was scooped and the sleeves were long giving way to transparency just past the elbows. It was the color of the sea and with every movement changed into shades of deep blues and pale greens. As I moved the gown, it reminded me of the tide rolling in and out. I was speechless. It was the most beautiful thing I had ever seen in my life and she had handed it to me.

I couldn't help the tears that flowed. She quickly handed me some tissue and instructed me to blot my eyes. She to was crying. We hugged and she helped me get into the dress. I needed a moment to myself. I finally had the courage to look in the full length mirror. I still didn't recognize the person before me. No more a scrap of a girl eight years old running in the shadows, in its place an attractive young women. When had I left my childhood behind and become this person I thought?

Leaving her room I entered the main room where Ethel, Ethan and Sanna were waiting. We bid Ethel goodbye, and off we went. As Ethan had said, "The best looking man with the two best looking gals. I'll be the envy of the party." I knew he was being nice, but the way he looked at Sanna told me he appreciated her in more ways than one tonight.

Down the path we strolled toward the ceremonial grounds. My apprehension growing with every step.

Chapter 15

Ceremony
Leon

I had gone to Sanna's that morning and the lot of them were gone. Ethel was watching the little ones. She told me they had to get supplies. I was frustrated. I wanted to spend time with her. Raoul had questions I was to ask. Now what? I couldn't help feeling exasperated. I assessed my situation and ran my fingers through my hair. I decided I would head into town to get my robes for tonight and my errands done.

In town I ran into Ethan. He was headed into the carpenters shed. "Where's Raina?" I blurted out a little to angry. I wasn't upset with him. I was upset at the circumstances.

He winked at me, "Shopping with your sister. Good luck separating her from Sanna." I knew he was right. Sanna would get her way. If she wanted Raina with her, she would keep her. I would just have to wait.

"When will they be back?" I questioned.

"Probably around lunch time. Do you want me to tell Sanna your coming over?" Ethan replied.

I ran my hand thru my hair and replied, "No, I have to meet with Raoul then. Maybe after?"

"Nope, Sanna has her roped into the ceremony tonight; and I am not going to be the one to tell Sanna that Raina can't go." Ethan was waving his finger at me and shaking his head no. I didn't blame him. Sanna was a tough one to argue with. He was a brave man for marrying her.

I ran my hands across my face. Defeated. "You wouldn't know if she is one of us would you?"

"Sanna knows more about her past, but what she shared with me, I would think not. Came from a regular village on the West coast somewhere. We don't know of any packs or villages like ours that way. You should ask Sanna though. Hey, I got to go. See you tonight then."

"Yeah, see you then." I walked away headed to my next errand before meeting Raoul.

It was just after lunch as I strolled to the Atheneum. Raoul was waiting. I was eager to find out what he had learned. There were so many questions. I was still in a foul mood from not being able to talk with Raina myself. To top it off, Sanna knew more about her then I did. Frustration was eating at me.

I made it to the door and ran down the winding staircase. Raoul was waiting for me at a table filled with books. Some open, some in piles. I sat down across from him in one of the fine leather crafted chairs that filled the Atheneum. Quietly I waited for him to start.

"Finding answers has proved to be a challenge." Raoul stated. "There is very little knowledge on the Koboldrone. I would like to speak with her tomorrow."

"I will see what I can do. Are you to say, that we have no more answers then we did before." I asked.

Raoul rubbed his chin. "Is she one of us?" He asked patiently.

"No, what does that mean?" I said with anxiety in my voice.

Raoul continued to rub his chin. He began shifting books and opening to marked pages within. Turning a dusty torn book around, he pointed to a passage. "I had originally thought," he started in a calculated and thought provoked statement, "if she was one of us." He paused. "Perhaps, you were not fully captured into the spell, allowing for her scent to arouse your mating desire. The animal in you awakened was enough to break the spell on your soul." Raoul rubbed his chin some more and tapped to the pages in front of me.

"But that is not the case is it?" I replied asking myself as much as I was asking Raoul. "How is it that she was not affected by the Koboldrone?"

We went around in circles, asking questioning, searching, theory after theory being disproved. Nothing made sense. The more we searched, the more questions Raoul and I had.

"I wonder." Raoul spoke to himself. He left the table and went in search of a book. I sat waiting for him to return. He arrived back with a small white leather clad book. It had strange writings on the spine. I did not know what language it was. Raoul set it on the table and began searching the pages. It looked from my angle to be genealogy charts. I was confused how this would help us. I stood up and began to pace. We had no more answers then when we started. Raoul continued flipping thru the pages.

Raoul whispered again, "I wonder?"

I practically screamed at him, frustration mounting, "What do you wonder?"

"This is the record of when magic came to be. The first holders and conductors of magic. Alaric was a wise man who lived over 600 years ago. In his travels he discovered a way to manipulate and alter his reality. He knew this gift should not be given to only one man. He went about teaching and sharing this gift with others. Some he taught the power to fly. Others he taught the powers to shift. To some potions and talismans, others teleportation. Never teaching any person or group, more than a single gift. Alaric in his wisdom wanted there to be balance.

Generation after generation passed, all living in peace. He married in his old age and had a son and a daughter. All his knowledge was passed by the fates only to his son, unbeknownst to Alaric. When Alaric found out, he bound his son, Latif, from using his magic. Eventually Alaric died and with it the bind that held his son. His son gained an instant knowledge of all things.

Latif was a powerful, yet kind wizard. Only doing good. He married and had two boys. Each son gaining the knowledge and power as he did. Unlike his father, he did not bind his sons. He taught them how to use magic. Eventually Latif died. In his place as wizard, left his sons, Alastair and Nezra. Nezra was jealous of his brother. He sought to kill him. As far as anyone knows he did. It has been over 200 years. It is said Nezra used his magic to extend his life. Upon the death of his brother he became more powerful than his grandfather ever was." Raoul took a slow breath then looked back at the charts that had ended.

"What became of the daughter of Alaric?" I asked.

Raoul shook his head. "According to the charts, she died young. Drowned in the river. Her father could not save her from death.

"And Alastair, any children?" I wanted to know.

"A single unknown named daughter. She is shown to be ungifted. It also says she married a young man according to the book then nothing more is mentioned. That was over 100 years ago." Raoul commented.

"So, how does this help us with answers?" I asked, still confused as to why we went off on this tangent.

Raoul leaned forward in his chair and said, "When I was a boy my grandfather had told of a traveler that came to our village. He taught us how to make the potions and talismans that we use today. I wonder if the same happened to her village, if they were taught by the traveler how to break curses." Raoul sat quietly rubbing his chin. "My grandfather always thought it was Alastair who ventured into his village. Swore he looked liked this." At that Raoul turned the book toward me and I saw the picture he was pointing to. I stared at the drawing. His green painted eyes staring back at me. Raoul looked from me to the book. Confusion was still etched over my face.

He said, "I'm afraid I have nothing more to say. This may be the best answer to your question." He paused. "It is time for you to get ready. The ceremony will be starting soon. Please, bring her by tomorrow." Then he rose from the table book in hand and left.

I sat for a moment. Mind spinning. If her village had that ability, maybe they could share their knowledge. It would be a great argument against the council to get them to let her stay. I thought of our past conversations. Why didn't she just tell me she knew how to break the curse? It was no big deal. I felt there was more involved. I looked at the wooden clock on the wall and noticed how late the hour was. If I didn't hurry I would be late myself to the wedding.

Where were they! The crowd had grown larger and still no sign. I sat in my chair at the head of the Council members frantically scanning the crowd and paths that led to the event.

Here I was waiting at the ceremony. Where were they! That's all I could think about. If I knew my sister, she would have made sure that Raina didn't back out and would be here tonight. Nothing delighted Sanna more then playing dress up. Tonight would be the ultimate playground for my sister. Raina didn't know what she was in for. Since talking to Ethan and Raoul, I have felt nothing but edgy, anxious, and some would say down right Asbjornish today. Now, I was waiting. Why weren't they here yet?

I could see the bride and groom coming down the path. It wouldn't be long before the events of the evening started. I glanced around as casually as I could eyeing the crowd for the set. Off to my side I heard the familiar laugh of Sanna. I turned my head in the direction of the sound. Coming gracefully down the path arm in arm was Sanna and Ethan. Raina's not with them. I was puzzled. I felt relief that she had not come and disappointment that I would not see her. Then as the couple turned the crook in the path, Raina was there. Walking a few paces behind them. She was beautiful. A siren of the sea. I couldn't take my eyes off her.

The music had began. The couple on the platform starting the dance. I saw Sanna, Ethan, and Raina stop at a table on the other side of the court. Sanna was introducing her to her acquaintances and some young eligible men. I began feeling possessive as I watched. Then our eyes met. A smile crept over her face giving me hope. It wasn't until I felt the elbow to my gut from Elder Raoul that I realize it was time to begin. I kept my eyes fixed on the couple, not wanting to look at Raina and be distracted. I stepped forward as the song ended. Clearing my throat and centering myself in front of the couple, I began the rehearsed traditional ceremonial speech.

"We are here at the invitation of Courtney and Brennon. They have confessed there love for one another and sought permission from the council to move forward in matrimony. Sealing themselves together for all time and eternity."

As I looked into the crowd. I locked eyes again with Raina. Unable to break away as I professed the couples love. "They will love, honor, respect, protect and care for each other till the ends of time. They have been matched in the sacred tradition of true love. Forever to be bonded....." I repeated the oaths and finally was able to break my bond with Raina to look at the glowing couple. It was time for the test. I graciously introduced Elder Raoul. Then stepped back into line at the edge of the half circle of Elders.

The enchantment drifted up like wisps of perfume. Entangling its vines around the couple. Then drifted into the crowd to enchant those of age. My hand reached up and absently stroked the talisman I wore around my neck. Normal traditions didn't apply to me as chief. When the council felt a mate was required, they would provide a selection to compete for the honor. I glanced at Elder Raoul as he came to stand by me. He looked at my hand stroking the talisman. With a nod of his head he held out his hand for me to remove it.

I slipped it from around my neck and handed it over. With in minutes I felt as if I was floating in the air. I wandered through the crowd. There were no faces, no people, only pillars of pink fire. I knew they were women, but continued walking past each one. I heard the crowd cheer. Relieved the couple had found one another. I didn't care where I was headed or who, if anyone, I would ask to dance. I let my animal instincts lead the way. Ready to embrace any distraction I could get from my feelings for Raina.

I felt compelled to stop. In front of me a green lit flame. It was memorizing to watch. Giving way to tradition. I asked the person of this light to dance. What harm would it do I thought.

Chapter 16

Dance

Raina

The grounds were beautiful. Low floating orbs of light no bigger than my hand were hanging just above the crowds. Vines of flowers and ivy created columns in a circle separating the woods from the center of the grounds. A platform decorated in strange metallic symbols stood in the center surrounded by more columns with white flowers and ivy making an inner circle. Upon the platform a couple dressed in white danced. Behind the platform at the edge of the outer ring was a stand with velvet soft high back chairs. Sitting upon them, I guessed was the Council.

As I looked across each man standing in front of his chair at the end was a face I recognized. Leon. He looked straight at me. Sanna was introducing me. All I could do was look back at Leon. A smile ran across my face. I felt the heat in my cheeks as I blushed. His gaze was broken by the older man standing next to him. I looked down at the ground working to rid myself of the butterflies in my stomach. When I had enough courage to look up again, he was walking toward the platform and the couple.

The music stopped, the couple faced toward Leon. He had everyone's attention and began to address the crowd. As he did, I felt he was only talking to me. I knew that couldn't be true. Nonetheless, I couldn't tear my gaze away this time. When he did break my gaze, I stepped back a few feet, and behind another women eager to hide my emotions. From the shadows I watched the festivities.

Sanna leaned back and began instructing me on the happenings of the ceremony. I saw the currents of colorful vines wrap around the groom. Then venture out into the crowd, wrapping their arms around each person. My gown went from vibrant turquoise to black. I gasped at the sight. All the beautiful colorful gowns in the crowd were black. The bride stood in the center, then in a wisp of pink fire disappeared. She was gone. I looked quizzically at Sanna. She whispered back, "Time for him to find her. The test has began."

We watched in silence as he moved from group to group placing a hand on the shoulder of a random person then taking in a deep breath. His head would shake and he would move on. I watched as he did the same to Sanna. Breathed her in, let go. He had moved halfway around the circle when he took a person by the hand and escorted her to the main platform. He announced his choice. I held my breath for him. Awaiting for the mark that the test was passed. In silence the whole crowd hovered. The elderly Councilor that began the test stepped onto the platform for a second time. He chimed a few words I could not decipher. Then the ground appeared to be on fire. Colors of every kind burst from the ground into the night sky. The flames dispersed and standing in the center were the bride and groom, again dressed in white. The crowd cheered. The music began again. I slunk back into the shadows of the Forrest. Away from the crowds and celebration.

I was enjoying myself, but had thoughts of tomorrow on my mind. I did not want to upset the joyous celebration. The crowd was beginning to dance. I saw Sanna and Ethan enter the dance floor. Her gown, like the others, back to the original purple hues that matched her eyes. The music was compelling. Watching, I decided I would head back to Sanna's. I would let them enjoy the evening. I pushed off the tree I was leaning on and turned to follow the path we had come from, when I met Leon's eyes.

I hadn't noticed him coming, it took me by surprise. I just stood there. Not sure what to say or do. He bowed and extended his hand.

"Dance with me?" He asked politely.

I didn't know what to do. I didn't dance. I had to many emotions going through my body at that moment looking at him in his perfection. I didn't think I could trust myself, not to like him more than I already knew I did.

"I don't know how to." Hoping that would deter him to ask another.

He leaned in close to my ear. I could feel the heat of his breath on my cheek. I felt my knees start to collapse. With a hand on my waist holding me up he whispered, "I will teach you. Let me."

I placed one hand in his and one on his shoulder as I had seen Sanna do with Ethan. Clumsily following his steps, I tripped and stumbled through the dance. After a short time, I stopped. Looking into his eyes, I shook my head.

"I can't do this." I was whispering to myself as much as I was telling him.

He leaned down to me, cheek next to mine. "You will get it. Let me help you." He pulled me closer. My body now modeled to his. I laid my head on his chest and listened to the beat of his heart. It calmed my nerves. Slowly we started again. I felt so secure and safe in his arms. I felt the music surround us as we hovered in the shadows, I was following his movements. I was dancing.

I don't know how long we had danced but when we stopped, my body went cold from the release of his touch. He looked down at me, his hands on my shoulders. I looked down to the ground, embarrassed now that I had been so comfortable in his arms. He lifted my face with a hand on either side of my cheeks, and kissed me.

Soft and gentle at first. Then with a growing urgency it deepened. Filling my body with warmth from head to toe. My arms betrayed me and slid up his chest then tangled into his hair. It was Leon who slowed the kiss. Leon gently pushed me back to look at my face. The song ended then. Surprise and delight flickered for a brief moment. Then the serious hard unreadable face I had not seen before set into place. He unlatched the locket from my neck and slipped the pendent into his jacket pocket. Turned, and headed through the woods back to the ceremonial crowd.

I stood there flushed and trembling. Hands on my neck were the locket had been. My mind going a hundred miles an hour. I heard Sanna calling my name, saw her coming my direction. I couldn't look at her, couldn't watch him walk away anymore. I turned and ran all the way back to Sanna's, tears running down my cheeks.

I walked into the house. Ethel was there. The children were already down for the night. She didn't ask any questions, just helped me get changed. I put on my original black outfit. Sanna had one of the vendors stitch and repair the rips and holes in my clothes. I wanted to be ready to leave first thing in the morning.

When I was ready, Ethel gave me a hug and went on her way. I found my spot by the fire and closed my eyes. Hours later, I heard Sanna and Ethan enter the house. She walked over to me and laid her hand on my shoulder. "If you want to talk I am here" she whispered. Then quietly they went into their room and shut the door. I let the tears come back. The rejection from Leon stung my heart. Sleep soon came.

I was up before the sun. I had tossed and turned all night. Decided I would get going instead of battle a sleep that would not be. I gathered the children one by one, placing the sleeping babes in the cart. I had just put Wyatt in the canopy, when I heard a throat clear behind me. It was Sanna. Her hair was wild. Her eyes still sleepy. I smiled at her.

"Sneaking out are we?" She asked with one eyebrow raised.

"Didn't want to wake you all." I replied.

"Wait! I have something for you."

"No, you've given us so much already, it's not necessary."

At that she disappeared into the house and came out seconds later with a small box in her hands.

"I couldn't." I said.

She opened the box. Inside was a small wooden oval with symbols carved into the wood. It was attached to a leather band. She pulled the necklace out with one hand, set the box down, and tied it around my neck. I ran my fingers over the decorative piece of wood.

"I couldn't." I repeated.

"This will help you," she choked out, tears in her eyes. "It will allow you to know what shifters are saying when they are transformed. Help you decipher good from bad intentions. You must keep it."

I smiled and thanked her, tears now running down our cheeks. We hugged. I turned to walk down the steps to my cart. When her throat cleared again. Looking back, Sanna was shaking her head at me.

"Forgetting something are you?" She asked me.

Confused I replied, "No, I don't think so."

"Ethan! Time!" and stumbling out of the house still putting his shirt on came a sleepy eyed Ethan.

"Now your ready." She smiled at me and turned back into the house.

I looked at Ethan ready to tell him to stay, but he beat me to the cart.

"If you want to argue with her go ahead, otherwise let's get going." He said with a smile at Sanna's back.

The five of us headed out, Ethan pulling the cart. We walked in silence to the edge of the land. It had been hours. The sun was just now breaking over the horizon. I hugged him goodbye, then turned and continued down the path alone.

Chapter 17

Questions

Leon

I didn't see her again the rest of the night. Instead I got disapproving looks from my sister. She didn't understand. I eventually moved so I would no longer see Sanna staring at me. I had enough on my mind as it was. I needed to talk with Raina. Raoul and I needed to talk to Raina. We needed answers. We needed confirmation to our theory. My mind raced. I would go see her first thing in the morning.

The ceremony was winding down. People began to leave. The couple gone hours before. It was my duty to see that all the guests would make it home. No funny business late at night. I had seen to my duty, then headed home myself. It was a few hours before the sun would be up. I needed to get some rest before starting a new day. I lay on my bed, my mind drifted to a few days ago, when I had seen Raina sitting by my bedside, hand on my chest. The memory brought back the feel of her hand. I decided, she would no longer stay at Sanna's, but would stay with me till she was required to leave. With this new information, I could go back to the council and argue with them to allow her to stay.

My mind switched to the events of tonight. Why did I choose her to dance with? Why did I feel so strongly to kiss her? When we were dancing, I felt so compelled to keep her in my arms. I had convinced myself during the dance that it was in no way Raina. How could it be? She was not one of us. When the desire came to kiss her. I welcomed the distraction. Hopeful it would lead me to someone else. A possible mate. The words from Raoul's first theory about us being fated together; that her scent awakened the beast within entered my mind. Could we be fated? How could one be fated to one not of there kind? It didn't make sense. It had never happened before that I knew of. More questions. Always more questions.

The sun was coming up now. I still did not sleep. My brain racked with to many thoughts. I dressed for the day. Stood at the door ready to go to Sanna's. I had to stop myself. Sanna was already mad at me for some unknown reason. The last thing I wanted to do was wake her up. She was not an early bird. I didn't want the morning wrath to land on me. So I sat, staring into a cold fire with only my thoughts.

It was finally a decent enough hour to go knocking on Sanna's so I headed out. When I got there, I could see the fire going, and hear the sounds of muffled voices. My timing was good. I walked up the steps to her home and opened the door.

I saw Sanna standing over the stove cooking. She didn't turn around. Ethan was sitting on a chair consoling Sasha who was wailing. I looked around the room. Panic settled in my stomach.

"Where is Raina and the children?" I asked. Nobody answered.

"Where is Raina?" I demanded!

Sanna spun around spoon waging at my chest. Anger and tears in her eyes.

"She is gone. Started her journey." She said sarcastically.

"Seriously, where is she?" I demanded again.

"I told you, what do you care anyway. The way you treated her last night, now you care, or is it your council that's asking, making sure she is gone. What! Did she not leave fast enough for you all?" She scolded me.

I was panicked and shocked.

"We needed to talk....I needed to talk... I didn't try to hurt her ... where is she?" I stammered out.

"I saw her to the border hours ago. She is headed up the Wiley trail toward the rock face path." Ethan answered.

"I need to get her." I said, hand in my hair. I turned to leave the house. Sanna was now blocking the door. "Move" I commanded. She did not, "Move or I will move you." I yelled.

"Leon, you are not going to drag her back here just so you can torture her with your questions. I will not allow it." Sanna threatened back.

"You don't understand, move." I was feeling desperate. She was going to be gone and I may not find her.

"Make me understand!" Sanna commanded.

"Fine." I ran my fingers into my hair. I took a chair by Ethan. Sanna stayed between me and the door. So, I told them what had happened. How I awoke, followed Raina. The children being awaken from the Koboldrone. Then looking at Sanna, I told her about the dance.

"I didn't know it was her." I stated. "I thought it was just a random maiden in the village, that it would ease my tension and take my mind off what was going on. When the enchantment broke and I saw I was kissing her, I didn't know what to do." I was pleading with my sister now. Seeking her guidance.

"I have questions, Raoul has questions, I need to know if we are fated together or if this feeling will pass." I put my head in my hands then, exasperated at the retelling. Sanna stood there silently a soft smile rounding her lips.

"Do you love her?" she asked.

"I don't know, I know I want to protect her and the children. I know I want her to be around." Lifting the locket out of my pocket I dangled it in front of my eyes, "I know I don't want anyone else to be with her."

Sanna gasped at the site of the necklace. She stepped to me and put a hand on my shoulder. "You should keep that. Ethan and I will go with you up the Rosa pass. We can drop

Sasha off at Ethel's then we can talk about what we know of Raina. If she stayed on the path, you should be to her just after sunset." Sanna paused then. "She has had a hard life. You need to be certain that she is your mate. That this is what you want. I don't want to see her hurt anymore."

"I won't hurt her." Was my reply. Sanna was right, maybe I did love her. Maybe we were fated. I waited for Sanna to get ready. Then we took off running out the door and up the path. Once Sasha was dropped off, Sanna began telling me all about Raina as we ran.

Chapter 18
Goodbye
Raina

The kids were doing great. The presents Sanna had given them were making the time fly for the children. I had also made good time. Running with the cart when the children were sleeping, and keeping them moving when they were awake. We only stopped to relieve ourselves. That was minimal at most.

I pulled out some dried meat for us to eat for dinner. Dinner, like lunch and breakfast, was eaten as we walked. The quicker we got to our destination, the safer I would feel. I was fishing around the basket of meat, when my fingers brushed a box. I didn't recall putting any boxes in this basket. I wrapped my fingers around it, and pulled it out. It was a plain brown box the size of my fist. I opened it. Inside was a folded note.

'If you find yourself in need of help, give a whistle - S.'

A smile lit my face. Sanna was still looking out for us. I tucked the whistle into my waistband pocket, then fished out some dried meat and we continued walking as we ate.

Nightfall had come. The children had settled into the cart some time earlier. They were now fast asleep. The path

I was on, was smooth and had been well traveled. There was no one in site. Hadn't been for a few hours now. The moon was high in the sky, casting much light onto the path. My plan was to walk well into the night, rest for a few hours, then begin again before the children awoke.

The trees were clustered together in lumps no longer packed like the woods of Ladow. The path we were on was lined with high tangled bushes, creating a tunnel with there branches. Behind the bushes, clear landscape with small huddles of thick trees spread about. I walked along in silence.

A slow creeping chill started rising up my spine. I was getting the feeling we were being followed. I looked behind us, nothing. After a good hour, I still couldn't shake the feeling. I veered off the path, through the bushes out of sight. I continued to walk. I could still feel the uneasiness that we were not alone.

Ahead was a grove of tightly grown trees. A good hiding spot. I maneuvered the wagon into the trees. It was well hidden. I gathered some broken bushes laying on the ground and moved them into the grove, adding to the coverage of the cart. When I stepped back, it was completely hidden. I ventured back to the path and stood in the bushes waiting, listening.

I heard the padding of feet coming down the path. Quietly I waited. Round the bend some distance off, a large copper wolf. He slowed down his trot and was walking slowly. He transformed into a large unkept, brut of a man. He had a torn shirt, with scratches and scars across his chest. He stopped. Looking behind him he whistled. A light tan scraggly wolf came out of the brush to his right.

"Do you smell them?" The larger one asked the scrappy wolf.

"No, they must have turned off somewhere." The wolf answered in reply.

"We can backtrack." He cackled.

I was unnerved by the sight. I patted the necklace I wore around my neck. I was grateful to understand this new threat. These men where up to no good. I needed to draw them away from the children. I planned my strategy. I could take them one at a time. The little scrappy one would be easy. The bigger one, would be tough. If I got some good swings in, I might be able to discourage him from following.

"Did you see 'em?" An additional black wolf came around the corner. "They can't be far, be a shame to give up such easy prey." The black wolf almost laughed as he said it.

"Enough, spread out and search, go back down the path and check for camps. We'll get them." The large one ordered.

I knew I needed to act. If I didn't, chances of them finding us all was inevitable. It would be horrific for the kids. I knew I couldn't take on all three at once. Now, chances of getting them one by one, was little to none. My only option, get them to follow me, lead them away, try to outwit them, circle back for the children. I knew I needed help. I ran toward the kids blowing the soundless whistle Sanna given me. I snuck into the grove. Gave one more blow then placed it into Keiko's tiny sleeping hand. As quietly as I could I took off toward the path, ran across it unseen, and headed in a large loop toward the back of the pack.

I was a good mile away from where I had left the children when I circled in toward the path. As I came close, I could hear them searching. I stood, waiting for a sign of the first to come. The black wolf came around the bend first. I whistled, catching his attention, then took off running through the groves of trees away from the path. Away from the children.

I looked backed once, he was so close. The other two now running to catch us. I ran down a hill, the landscape giving way to boulders, hills and ravines. I swerved between boulders, moving and jumping. I cornered a large boulder well above my height. Here I stopped. I held my daggers in hand, crouched low to the ground. When the black wolf turned to make the bend, I reached out for his throat slicing him from chin to belly. He collapsed immediately from the shock, but quickly regained himself and tried to roll away.

I jabbed my other dagger into his throat and turned the blade. His body convulsed then stopped. I pushed off the ground and ran. I could hear them. I heard a howl echo off the rock as they passed their dead comrade.

"Get her!"

All I could hear was them yelling for me. I ran up a hill. I hit a dead end, a cliff met my eyes. I skidded to a stop. Turning, I had a giant boulder to my right, to my left, an open valley. They would catch me in the valley. I couldn't out run them all. I scrambled to get to the top of the boulder. I might have a chance up there. I would wait them out if needed. So I scrambled up the boulder and posed, ready to defend my rock.

Chapter 19

Plan

Leon

It had been hours since I left Sanna and Ethan at the border. Thibault was on watch at this end of the valley. He was loyal to my father before me. A good man. When he saw us approach, he simply turned a blind eye to me as I walked over the creek that signaled our border. He could be trusted not to give away my plans. The sun would set soon, and still no sign of the group. I had hoped they would stop and rest along the way. Give me an opportunity to catch them. As I thought it, I knew Raina would push through. She wasn't one to waste time.

Night was here, the moon lighting the way. My worries growing with every hour. Then I heard the musical whistle. I knew this sound. It was Sanna's. Our father gave her this whistle when she was young. Our village was battling the southern pack. Sanna was scared that she would be taken and sold to the fortress.

Our father had this whistle made by our elders. Only our family could hear it. It played a soothing tone that would calm Sanna, and warn us of danger. She only used it once. She was walking back to our home with food from the market, when an Asbjorn crossed her path. She blew the whistle. My father was with me at the council chambers when we heard it. He immediately ran to her. He saved her from an awful state. She carried it with her for years, until the battles were won and over. I didn't see it again until his death. Now, I recognized the tone. She must have given it to Raina. Raina was in trouble. Why else would she activate the whistle.

I took off running as fast as I could. The tone, leading me to the place it was blown. As I turned a bend in the path, I saw Hagar running to the East, followed by his lackeys. They were in the thick of a chase. I watched waiting for their prey to appear. I saw Raina jump over a boulder leading them. My feet wouldn't move, the shock hitting me at once. I transformed and took off in chase. Following the trail of stench left behind by the pack.

I rounded a boulder and was met with a blood stained Yule. He was pushing his lifeless twin around. His snout covered in his brothers blood. He snarled at me.

"You did this!" He accused me. "You killed my brother!"

I knew it wouldn't matter trying to explain that I did not. Fact was it was probably Raina. I was glad she did. They were cruel, spineless, deflectors of our village. Out to seek power and glory. Now they gathered travelers to bargain with the Raiders. I had heard they were south of here. They shouldn't be this far north.

Yule and I were circling each other. I was waiting for him to pounce. I knew he would. He was no match for me, but he was wasting my time. I egged him on, wanting it to be over so I could help Raina.

It only took one insult about his brother to get him to pounce. The fight was on. I caught him under the throat. Bitting as hard as I could. He managed to get away. He came back. His skills improved from the last time we had fought. He got me under the front leg. Snapped it. I was hurt but not out. I grabbed his hind leg in my jaw and swung him around, hitting his head into the boulder behind me. He lay inches from his dead brother now. He moved to get up. I gave one last lung and tore his throat from his body. He was dead and no longer a threat.

I took off running best I could in the direction of Hagar. I could smell the trail. They were no longer moving. I made myself move faster. Raina, she needed to be alive. I came to a downward sloping hill. At the bottom, Raina stood on a boulder, arms swinging as Hagar, Mutt, and two others I did not recognize tried to climb the boulder. She was quick. Slicing snouts, or paws that made it up the rock. I crept close to the pack. No coverage to hide in. I was watching her. Then, she saw me. She looked, her head shaking, as if telling me to go back. I couldn't leave her. I crept closer. She hardened her face.

In that moment I knew what she was going to do. My heart broke in two, my fear coming out, I howled as she let her foot slide down the boulder in reach of Hagar. He snatched her down in one movement. Pinned her to the ground. The others circled towards me. I heard her yell,

"Kieko, Help them!" Then I saw as Hagar slammed his fist into her face. She no longer moved. Her eyes were closed. I growled ready to fight them all. Then the sound of the whistle hit my ears. Keiko was in trouble. I knew I needed to protect them, so I turned and ran to Keiko, Juji, and Wyatt.

"Coward, come back and fight." Hagar called after me. I heard him instruct the others. "Leave him. He is of no worth, we have a prize for the Raiders."

They did not follow me. I ran as fast as I could letting my instincts follow the whistle. The tone drifting in front of me like a trail of golden yellow smoke. I was close. I could feel them. Feel the magic of the whistle. It was close. All I could see was a small grove of trees. The ground fairly flat, with boulders in the distance. The grove ahead of me seemed to small for them. As I walked closer, I heard the soft cry of a child. I transformed myself back to a man. My arm, broken, I moved the brush out of the way. There Keiko was with a blade in hand ready to protect the children huddled behind her. She dropped the blade as our eyes met. The three scrambled into my arms. I grabbed them all and took off running back to the village. I had ran for close to a mile when I was met by Elder Gregory, Ethan, Sanna, and Thibault.

Sanna's eyes were wild. "Where's Raina?" she pleaded. I could only hang my head. Guilt filled me for letting her down. "Hagar" was all I could say without emotion taking hold. They took the children, we transformed and ran back to the village. I needed to make sure they were safe before hunting down Hagar. He would keep her alive, she was worth more to him alive than dead. That I was sure of.

It was sunrise when we stumbled into Sanna's home. I went for the lotion. Smeared it over my arm and headed for the front door. The children were safe, now I needed to get Raina.

I was stopped by Gregory. He had both hands on my shoulders pushing me down.

"What are you doing?" I questioned him. Ready to strike if needed.

"You are not being rational. You need a plan." Gregory responded.

"It's true," Ethan said. "What are you going to do, take Hagar and his pack down on your own? Besides, by the time you reach him, she will have been sold to the Raiders. You need a plan."

I threw my hands into the air, "What do you suggest, I sit here quietly waiting for her to just stroll through the village."

"No!" Sanna whispered, she was quiet and drawn in. The last time she was like this, our father had just died, and our mother had left. I began to worry for my sister.

Sanna continued, "I'm worried to. You need a plan that will bring you both home safely." She was sitting, staring into the unlit fire. Holding Wyatt as he slept. Ethel came out of the bedroom, took Wyatt and put him in bed with his sisters, and Sasha. Sanna stood and went to her room.

I looked at the others. Gregory was the first to speak. "I might have a plan. It's risky, but may work."

"Well, what is it." I screamed back. Then lowered my voice remember the children sleeping. They didn't need to be awaken. They had been through enough. I stared at him. "Well?"

"I know of some vendors who dabble from time to time with the Raiders. If I speak to them, maybe we could stage a capture. This would hide your true nature from the council. With luck your sell to the Raiders should put you both together. Then its up to you to escape with her in hand. The council cannot replace you as chief at least for five years according to our laws. Chances are, the Raiders wouldn't kill you on sight. If you both survive, it could work."

We all looked at him stunned. It was a horrible plan. It was the only one we had. It might work. If they were taking prisoners, then maybe she would be at the Raiders camp, not moved to the fortress yet. Easier to escape from there. I felt a bit of hope. Looking him in the eye, "Make it happen. I will wait here for you to return." At that Gregory left. Thibault, Ethan and I looked at each other.

"You crazy man." Thibault started. "Chances are she'll be dead before you reach her..."

I punched him in the jaw. I couldn't think that was a possibility.

Ethan stepped between us. "You know he is only looking out for you. This is a bad plan. At best you make it back alive. But when? Raoul was captured and sent to the fortress for three years before he escaped. He had help from the inside. Who do you have on the inside helping you."

I was pacing the room.

"Is she worth losing your life?" Ethan asked.

"Yes, I can't leave her there. I can't not try. What if it was Sanna?" I questioned back.

"If it was Sanna, I would take the chance." Ethan walked toward his room. Before entering he turned to me, "Get a good meal and some sleep Leon, it may be a while before you have that again. Good Luck."

Into the bedroom he went. I could hear a soft muted cry coming from Sanna.

"Ethan's right, eat and sleep. I will wake you when Gregory returns. We will keep an eye on things here for as long as you are gone." Thibault put his hand on my shoulder. He walked to the cooler grabbed some grub and shoved it my way. I ate till I was full, then sat in a chair. Thibault lit the fire. He chanted a few words, and I was soon asleep.

Sneak Peak
Book 2
The Guardian

Legends of Thaumaturga
The Guardian

H.C. MacDonald

Chapter 1
Fortress
Leon

The capture and brawl had gone off without a hitch. Ethan walked away with a black eye and light scratches. Gregory a broken arm. Thibault a split lip and cut leg. Nobody would suspect we weren't really attacked. I was taken as their prisoner. Our plan was working.

Gregory's acquaintances held up their end of the bargain and promptly sold me to the Raiders. I stayed in a partial transformation. I felt this would hide my identity, and allow me to be prized enough to be taken to the fortress instead of being killed on site. It worked. The Raiders liked the idea of me being there entertainment. Raina was not at the camp. Instead others like me were chained in cages, ready to be sent off.

I arrived days later. I was sore from all the bumps and dips the wagon took along the way. The fortress was large. A thick wooden gate with iron bars awaited our entrance. We were checked by the Raiders at the gate. Each adding their own insult my direction. Inside the courtyard I was re-shackled and dragged into the stone fortress building. As we walked, I tried to pick up on every detail. There were four guards at the gate. Two more on the walkway above the courtyard. Six more in the courtyard. We walked up one set of stairs, then down a long hall to another thick wooden door. There were to many guards to make an escape the way I had come. I would have to find another way.

The Raider at my front opened the heavy door. We were greeted with the smell of waste. I vomited in my mouth. A set of iron bars greeted us. He unlocked the second gate and thru me into a cell. I sat there alone in solitude for six months. My only visitor, Raiders, and that was just to bring me a meal from time to time.

One day they finally came to move me. He shackled my arms and legs, then waited for his companion to secure the area. They then took me to another stairwell. Out thru a large wooden door like before and an iron gate. We walked down a long hall. Either side of us were more cells. Each filled with a body. I didn't know if they were dead or alive. None looked our way.

"Put him in here." The raider in front of me chuckled.

"Ah, yes, she will make a tasty snack for him." The one behind me said as he unlocked the cell door.

I snarled at them both, playing my part. Then in an attempt to irritate them lashed out. I was immediately thumped across the chest. It knocked my breath out of me for a moment. I stumbled into the cell. My hope, that Raina was in this part of the fortress. The door closed and locked behind me. The Raiders laughed as they strolled down the hall and out the doors.

I knew it wasn't Raina. I could smell it. Slowly I turned. Growling and ready to fight. Hidden in the corner in the shadows and a pile of dirty hay was a young girl. No more then twelve. She was very thin, and scared. I immediately stopped growling. I moved to the bench that hung from chains on the wall and sat.

"I won't hurt you." I said to the shadow.

Slowly, she moved out of the corner. She came to sit in front of me between the bench and the door.

"What is your name?" I asked.

"Kayley." Her voice was a mere whisper. She looked at me. Then down at the cell floor. Opting to draw on the rocks with a piece of straw. I watched her silently. Thinking what my next steps would be, this plan to escape had been taking to long. Now that I had been moved, this might be the chance I needed to get out, and find Raina.

Hours passed, neither of us saying a word. My stomach growled. My hunger was getting to me through my boredom. "Do they feed us?" I broke the silence with my question.

"Sometimes." Kayley answered. She had been playing with the piece of straw for hours. I laid on the bench with one arm under my head.

"Is there a way out of here?" I figured we had the time, and I needed more information to formulate a plan.

"My friend may know a way." She replied.

"Is your friend here?" I asked starting to feel frustrated. She was not very forthcoming with answers.

"Maybe." She said.

I ran my hand thru my hair. "Can I talk to her?"

"That's up to her." Was my reply.

Okay, I thought, let's try a different line of questions. Maybe that will get us somewhere. "How often do the guards come in?"

"Sometimes every day, sometimes twice a day, sometimes not at all." Kayley said.

"Do they always come in pairs?"

"No."

"So they come alone sometimes."

"Yes."

I felt a little hope. If one came alone, opened the cage or got close enough for me to grab hold of. Maybe with the help of the others here, I could get loose. Find Raina, then head home.

"Do you know any of the others here."

"No, they sleep mostly."

I was feeling frustrated again. This was going to take time. I stood up to pace the cell. I needed to have a plan. I was at the end of our cell facing the moldy stone wall deep in thought when I heard the sound of an iron door move. I moved to the bars and looked through the cells to the doors I had come through. No one was there. I moved back into the shadows of my cell. I heard the noise again. My back was to the bars. As I stood there, I smelled the familiar scent I had come to know Raina by. It was very faint. Hard to decipher from the other stenches that filled the floor I was on. A flutter of relief filled me. She was here somewhere. I heard the young girl move closer to the bars.

"You have a guest." I heard Raina's voice say. I turned from the wall to face the cell bars. Beyond the iron cage sat Raina. She was covered in dirt and wore a burlap sack tied at the shoulders. I could see a fresh cut across her collar. Anger swelled up inside me. I watched as she handed the girl two rolls of bread. With a smile she added, "Tell him the rules. We don't want anyone to get hurt. Three days to the arena event, keep your head down."

The young girl smiled up at her. "I can do that."

"I know you can. I am counting on you." Was Raina's reply. She patted the girls hand and then stood to walk away. I wanted to go to her. For some reason I didn't. I stayed in the shadows. Afraid of her seeing me in this grotesque state I had transformed into. Afraid she would not remember me. I watched her as she gave each person a roll of bread. I could see the fresh whip marks on her back and scars on her shoulder. It looked as if someone had taken a knife and carved words into her back. I vowed to kill anyone who had done this to her.

Raina had just finished passing out all the bread she had brought and was headed back to the opposite end of the hall. As she passed our cell, I moved out of the shadows to the bars. She glanced at me and smiled. Then moved the iron grate that covered the wall and disappeared.

I was so relieved that she was alive. Together we could escape. I looked down at the young girl. She handed me some bread.

"Is that your friend?" I asked with a smile.

"Yes, she always brings us food when she can." She said stuffing the bread into her mouth.

"How long have you been here?" I asked her.

"A few months now." She took another bite. "My father and I were captured. Raina says he's okay and will be waiting for me. She can get you information if you need it. How long have you been here?"

"A while now. I hope to leave soon."

"I'm leaving soon. Raina says so." She said with a smile.

"How is that?" My curiosity peaked. Did Raina already have a plan. She was resourceful, and from what my sister Sanna had told me, knew this fortress like the back of her hand. If anyone knew how to slip by the guards, she did. I felt a surge of hope grow inside me. I knew a plan would come together. "So what are these rules of yours?" I asked my host.

"First, don't upset the guards. If you do, you will go to the Arena. Raina can't help you there. Second, if you do go to the arena, run as fast as you can to the gate. It is only open for a short time. Three,.."

"Wait, why is the gate only open for a short time. Why do I need to run to it?"

"So you don't get killed. That's what Raina says." She was so absolute in her answer I dared not question her again.

"Three, whatever she tells you to do you do. No questions. Got it."

"Yes, ma'am." I replied. These were easy enough rules. Considering number one, my plan to take down the guard was canceled. I needed to trust Raina. If she did have a plan, that was good enough for me.

Legends of Thamaturga

© Copyright 2016, H.C. MacDonald

Rights Reserved.

    This document may be downloaded for personal use; users are forbidden to reproduce, republish, redistribute, or resell any materials from this document in either machine-readable form or any other form without permission from HC MacDonald or payment of the appropriate royalty for reuse.

Made in the USA
Middletown, DE
26 November 2016